Puffin Books

The House G

'He wanted to go back. Yet he knew it was crazy to go back . . . And if he did . . .'

The HBS is getting better and better at its dangerous games. Gunno, Jess, Wally and Pete make a great team – until the fateful day when they discover the old secluded house in the valley. After that, nothing is the same again. For there's something very strange about this house, something waiting, something that compels Gunno to return again and again . . .

The House Guest was winner of the 1992 Australian Children's Book of the Year Award (Older Readers), winner of the 1992 SA Festival Award for Literature (Children's Books), and winner of the 1992 Victorian Premier's Literary Award (Children's Books).

'a powerful novel . . . Nilsson tells a story worth telling in a book which older readers will undoubtedly agree is worth reading.'

Adelaide Advertiser

Also by Eleanor Nilsson

Parrot Fashion
The Rainbow Stealer
Tatty
A Bush Birthday
Heffalump?
The 89th Kitten
Pomily's Wish
Heffalump? and the Toy Hospital
The Black Duck
A Lamb Like Alice

Non-fiction

Writing for Children

The House Guest

Eleanor Nilsson

Puffin Books

Puffin Books
Penguin Books Australia Ltd
487 Maroondah Highway, PO Box 257
Ringwood, Victoria 3134, Australia
Penguin Books Ltd
Harmondsworth, Middlesex, England
Viking Penguin, A Division of Penguin Books USA Inc.
375 Hudson Street, New York, New York 10014, USA
Penguin Books Canada Limited
10 Alcorn Avenue, Toronto, Ontario, Canada M4V 3B2
Penguin Books (N.Z.) Ltd
182-190 Wairau Road, Auckland 10, New Zealand

First published by Penguin Books Australia, 1991
First published in Puffin, 1993
10 9 8 7 6 5 4

Typeset in Bembo by Typeset Gallery, Malaysia
Printed and bound in Australia by The Book Printer, Victoria

National Library of Australia
Cataloguing-in-Publication data:

Nilsson, Eleanor, 1939-
The house guest.

ISBN 0 14 034 601 5

I. Title.
A823.3

Acknowledgements
The extract from Walter de la Mare's poem 'The Truants' is reproduced with kind permission from the Literary Trustees of Walter de la Mare and the Society of Authors as their representative.

Excerpts from *A Wizard of Earthsea* by Ursula Le Guin, copyright © 1968 by The Inter-Vivos Trust for the Le Guin Children, are reprinted by permission of the Houghton Mifflin Company.

To Lochie and her house
and
in memory of my brother,
Murdoch Stewart Luke

I wish to express my sincere gratitude to the Literature Board of the Australia Council whose kind assistance enabled me to complete this book.

I would also like to thank my friend Helen Stafford for her many patient and helpful readings of the manuscript.

Chapter One

It had almost been too easy. They hadn't been sure whether to do it or not, at first. Indeed they'd nearly had a quarrel about it. Not that they ever really quarrelled. Jess saw to it that they didn't.

They'd been working on the plan. Jess and the others brought him the information, and Gunno drew it up. He liked drawing and diagrams and it was easier to follow when he did it. So usually they just left it to him. But when they'd filled him in on this one he'd balked at it. 'I'd give it a miss,' he said.

'Why, Gunno?' asked Jess, giving him all her attention. She relied on Gunno's advice – he'd often been right in the past.

'It's big,' he said briefly. 'It's near the main road.'

'But on the side,' said Pete, 'there's lots of trees. No one'd see.'

'Alarms?' suggested Gunno. 'House as big as that?'

Wally chipped in. 'Wire screens are all going. Needs a paint. There wouldn't be an alarm.'

Jess nodded and ticked the house off on her sheet. 'We'll be extra careful there, Gunno,' she said, 'but it sounds all right. Place like that's usually good.' She patted him placatingly on the shoulder, her long hair swinging round and brushing against his cheek.

He shifted on his chair. 'All right.' He started drawing in the house on the plan, but quickly, angrily, almost. 'Just the same, you're starting to take risks.'

'It's all risks,' said Pete indignantly. 'When isn't it?'

'Some risks are unacceptable.'

'"Unacceptable",' piped up Wally. 'What sort of language is that?'

'Perfectly good language,' said Jess, 'and better than the stuff you come up with. And Gunno's right – we mustn't get cocky.'

Yet the thought came to her that Pete and Wally were somehow right too when they complained about his language. Gunno was cool, very cool, and sensible. Good on the job when the others got flustered. But there was something dreamy about him – something maybe to do with using words like 'unacceptable'. She didn't know quite what she meant, but sometimes she had the feeling that Gunno might one day prove to be a problem. She watched him working on the map – neat, methodical, absorbed. He had nice hands, she thought, looking at them properly for the first time. Sensitive-looking, as though he'd play the piano or something dumb like that – not be roaming the neighbourhood with the HBS. His hair was nice too – dark and thick and curling in slightly at the back. She sighed and went back to her list.

They had met at Gunno's house. That was breaking a rule, really, but Pete said it was too stinking hot to go to the park so they'd met there. Gunno's father was out all day and sometimes half the night as well, for he had two jobs, so it was safe enough as far as that went. And they'd turned up at different times. They were always careful about details, the HBS. Jess had decided it was safer rather than not seeing one another at all out of school to see each other occasionally – to appear mildly friendly so that if they did have to get together unexpectedly no one seeing them would do a double take. But usually, almost always, at least until recently, they met in scrub quite a bit in from the lake at the National Park.

It was in the National Park that they had met that first time. That time too they'd arrived at different times, even Wally and Pete, for it could look suspicious going around with your brother all the time or even too often. So, separately, they'd ridden their bikes to the lake, then left them in the scrub and headed north along the big track that quickly dwindled to a narrow one; past bushes and bushes of African daisy that blazed yellow in spring, over the creek bed and past a scruffy melaleuca hedge to a small cleared space between three huge red gums that marked their spot. They'd lain in the dry grass, looking up at the bright blue of the sky. Then while Pete had broken off all the black dead branches he could reach from last year's bushfire, Wally had chewed on barley grass and Gunno had stared comfortably into space, Jess had outlined the rules for what was to become the HBS.

'You have rules,' she had begun. 'You have strict rules and you stick to them.' Her voice had droned on with the flies, with the heat, but they had all listened. They always listened to Jess. That had been almost a year ago.

The house was fourth that morning. They'd done the three in MacAlister first. They'd watched them for a month – there was nothing sloppy about the HBS. But it had been harder to get the information on the big house. Wally said he'd watched it when he could for five weeks, to be extra sure, but there were two driveways, one leading out to the main road and one to MacAlister, and there was a big garden right round the house so that you couldn't get close to it.

'Still think it's risky,' said Gunno.

Yet, here they all were, in a grove of peppermints in a patch of the garden that bordered the dirt track off MacAlister, and apparently they were going to do it.

They always sent Wally to scout, because being younger, he looked cuter, still with soft features and fine floppy hair. He was good at excuses too – he varied them according to who came to the door – if anyone did. It hadn't happened often. 'I've lost my puppy,' he'd say to softish-looking people, or, and he'd be practically weeping, 'I've lost my white rabbit. He was there at teatime but he's gone this morning. Big ears.' He would make pathetic shapes of ears in the air in front of them, then, when the people shook their heads, he'd walk off up the path, his shoulders drooping. Or there was the all-purpose excuse to indeterminate-looking people: 'My dad's sent me to ask where the Gormans live.' Or, to the people ready to slam the door in your face before it was properly opened, 'Excuse me, but I was wondering if you'd like anyone to do jobs . . .' That was probably as far as he needed to go at a door like that.

But this time Gunno insisted on going himself. He was almost dizzy with nerves which wasn't the way he was used to feeling at all. He looked at the others. They seemed much as usual – Jess capable and calm, Pete a bit jumpy, and Wally as he always looked – a sort of failed version of Pete. They didn't seem to feel it then. But there was something about this job, this house, that made him uneasy – worse than uneasy – upset.

Jess hesitated, looked at him for a moment, then 'All right, you go, Gunno,' she said.

Gunno made the effort to pull himself straight and walk confidently down the pebbled driveway. 'Always act as if you have a perfect right to be wherever you are,' Jess was always telling them. 'Don't skulk.' That was all right – he could do that bit. But when he reached the red brick path – old bricks, old as this house was old – the swimmy feeling came over him again and his feet felt as if they weren't quite walking on the bricks, as he knew they were, but floundering somewhere above them. There was an old well that the bricks curved around in widening circles and a cement verandah with vines growing along the wires on the outside of it. He wasn't sure if he'd come to the front or the back door, but in any case, it was a door that he would have to try.

He opened the wire door. Wally was right. The wire in the top half section was pulling away. The beading at the bottom was falling off as well, for want of a nail or two. He was just about to rat-tat-tat confidently on the door when he felt it – someone was looking at him. He turned towards the window, but there was no face there peering at him through glass. Then he heard a snuffling noise, and he looked down. A dog's long pointed face was poking out of what must be a cat door. Gunno made himself go completely still. Blast Wally, he thought. He didn't say there was a dog. It had stuck its head right out now, out of the square hole, but it wasn't barking. Shivers ran up and down Gunno's back. It was like looking at a ghost dog – a dog that didn't bark at strangers. Yet the dog looked real enough, and nice-looking, what he could see. A really nice-looking gold and white and black dog. He dropped down to talk to it.

'Call yourself a watch dog,' Gunno reprimanded it, but gently. The dog stared at him, almost in a puzzled way, Gunno thought, with the kind of look that Jess often turned on him – when he'd said he didn't want to do this house, for instance.

He knew he should have gone then – why on earth hadn't he? There was a blasted dog, he hadn't wanted to come here anyway, yet something made him go on with it. He knocked on the door, first in an average sort of way, then loudly. The dog stared at him through the hole in the house, but still it didn't bark. It was uncanny. Gunno moved swiftly round the house then, looking in the windows where he could, knocking on the doors, trying handles, checking screens in his quick and practised way. Yet all the time he did it he knew the garden had that waiting feeling that told you the house was empty – empty apart from the dog.

Gunno walked back the way he had come. He only needed to say, 'There's a dog,' and that would be an end to it. Then again, there was something about this house . . .

'Well?' said Jess.

'There's a dog,' said Gunno, as he should have done.

Jess scowled, her green eyes going hard. 'I thought you checked this place out, Wally. Five weeks, you said.' *Rule 4: no dogs.*

'I never seen no dog,' said Wally, flushing.

'There's a dog all right,' Gunno repeated, then found himself adding, 'but it doesn't bark.' And reluctantly, in spite of himself, 'There's a door open.'

'Open?' said Jess, with a mixture of delight and outrage in her voice that Gunno could interpret quite easily.

He knew she was marvelling at the carelessness of people – a house like that, old stone work and goodness knows what inside – and they left it open. For anyone to walk in. Lucky it was only them . . .

She stood, weighing it up. A dog, but it didn't bark, and a door open. She took half a step forward.

'Oh come on,' said Pete, brushing past her. 'I'm going in.'

It was the side door on the secluded part of the house that was open: a glass door looking out onto trees and lawn with not another house in sight. Gunno walked in first, but slowly, almost on tiptoe as if the floor were hot. But it wasn't of course: the floor was made of broad pine planks, honey-coloured and cool. There was a wooden table on one side of the room, far longer than it was wide, and the walls around it were lined with books. He stared at them. Pete pushed past him and opened a door. Gunno could see vinyl: this room led into the kitchen, then.

All houses that were empty of their owners seemed hushed, but to Gunno this one seemed especially quiet. His uneasiness started to return. 'This is just the sort of house where there could be someone inside, tucked away in a distant room,' he whispered to Jess. And just as he'd said it a sharp series of barks rang out. Pete came running back, red-faced and swearing. He glared at Gunno. 'I thought you said it didn't bark.'

Jess pushed past them both. There was a stairway just outside the kitchen door, and on the top step stood the dog. It looked like a collie, but it was on shorter legs, with a sharper face, and smaller. Much smaller. It wasn't a big dog then – but what a noise it was making. At the sight of Jess as well as Pete and now Wally it had gone frantic. It was scared all right: its head and body flattening somehow at the same time as it was letting out all these defiant barks.

Jess thought quickly. 'We're in already,' she said. 'Let's just race through. Pete, go and bung it in a room.'

Pete leapt up the stairs two at a time.

'No,' said Gunno sharply, running after him. But it was too late. Pete shooed the little dog in front of him and when it wouldn't go he aimed a kick at one of its frail-looking legs. The dog stopped barking and cried a little, limping off. Pete shut the bedroom door on it and started work on the room opposite.

'You keep a watch, Wally,' said Jess, 'and I'll check the kitchen.'

Gunno sprang into the bedroom where the dog was.

It was cowering in a corner. He noticed with distaste that the bed hadn't been made – a big double one with two lots of pyjamas lying carelessly across it. He shut the window in case the dog started up again, and crouched down beside it. 'Hey, fella, it's all right. Pete didn't mean . . . You're all right.'

The dog stared up at him out of tragic brown eyes, liquidy-looking and almond in shape. They seemed to be full of reproach. This is crazy, Gunno thought. I'd better get on with it. I can't waste time on a dog. But everything he did seemed to be in slow motion. He started pulling out drawers. Sure enough, there was a maroon leather purse sitting right on top of everything else in the drawer next to the one that held make-up. Gunno sighed. People were so predictable. He pocketed some of the money and pushed the drawers back in. The one that held the purse was so stuffed with papers – timetables, old bills, Christmas cards, letters – that he had to rearrange them in order to shut the drawer. *Rule 2: leave everything as you found it.*

He checked the mattress, although he could tell without looking that they wouldn't be as subtle even as that. The dog was still watching him. It was starting to get on his nerves, the way it watched, but at least it wasn't barking. He glanced quickly round the room, then went out, closing the door behind him.

'Better be quick,' said Pete, emerging cheerfully from another room with a handful of notes, and at the sound of his voice the dog started barking again.

'You looked in here?' Gunno indicated the room at the top of the stairs. Its door was shut. All the other doors had been open.

'No,' said Pete. 'Better not press our luck. C'mon.'

Gunno went in anyway, interested by the shut door. But it was just another bedroom: a boy's room with cheery red and blue blinds with ships on them, a red quilt cover and a red-patterned carpet covering a part of the dark wooden floor. There was a smallish wooden desk with a single drawer and above it shelves littered with models, mainly of planes and space ships. A book was lying on a tiny table beside the bed. Gunno picked it up, glanced at it, then put it down again. He moved over to the bookshelf on the opposite wall.

Then he heard the sound of footsteps running up the stairs and Jess burst into the room. 'What on earth are you doing, Gunno? Can't you hear that dog?' She stared at the book in his hand. 'Books are no good, hardly ever. It'd be a good place to hide it but people never think of it. Come *on*, Gunno.'

He could tell she was thinking cool was cool, but that it was a bit too cool to be searching through the books. He didn't feel cool: he felt strange. The way he had felt on that brick path. Stranger than ever in this room. He looked round to check that she'd gone out again, then he shoved the book he was holding into an inside pocket of his jacket. He felt almost a chill as he did so, for he was breaking a rule, an important rule. *Rule 3: don't take anything but money, and don't take it all from any one place. No radios Pete, cassette recorders Wally, wallets Gunno. Only money.*

They'd disagreed about that rule, had a long discussion. Not that Gunno had disagreed: he'd agreed with Jess.

'Why not?' said Pete, challenging. He knew there were plenty of outlets for radios at least.

Gunno could tell from the way Jess hesitated that she had reasons but hadn't really thought them out. But now she settled down seriously to do so.

'We're professionals,' she had said at last. 'Not riff-raff. We're just creaming off a bit of the spare cash that lies around these places. They won't even miss it. And if we leave everything the way it was people might think they've imagined they had it. Or anyway, it'll take them longer to find out.'

'Talk about small time!' said Pete. 'No radios! And leave everything the way you find it you're gonna take double the time.'

'What do *you* think, Gunno?' Jess had asked.

Gunno knew she was relying on him to come up with something steadying. He had looked at her thoughtfully. 'People are upset if they're burgled,' he said at last in his slow way, 'but they care more about inconvenience and sentiment than petty cash – at least around here. They'd really worry about losing a credit card or even an old wallet that somebody gave them. They'll also be pleased that nothing's been disturbed. They'll feel *triumphant* that their video is still there or their flute or their typewriter. "Just kids", they'll say. They may not even bother to report it.'

Jess was smiling. That was just what she'd wanted to hear and maybe even what she'd half thought, but not, of course, in the sort of words that she would ever have chosen. Pete was glowering and Wally, as the youngest member, was keeping tactfully quiet, though he'd been listening all right, for later, out of this discussion, he'd come up with the name for their group.

Jess had smiled, pleased with him that day, Gunno remembered. Just the same, he was going to break the rule. He rearranged the books so that there was no gap on the shelves, and looked around him. Everything was the same as when he had come in. Yet there seemed to be something subtly wrong. Wrong with the room. He shook his head, puzzled. It *looked* all right.

'Gunno!'

It was Jess, again. He shut the door carefully behind him, then opened the window and the door of the bedroom where the dog was, and without registering it except as a dark shape in the corner, he ran down the stairs after the others. Even when they reached the dirt track he could hear the little dog barking furiously, endlessly, he was sure from the top of the stairs. It was funny, that, how it hadn't barked at first. It hadn't barked, he realised, when there had only been him.

Chapter Two

Sometimes Gunno was troubled by what he feared were obsessions. Something someone had said or done or that he had said or done would repeat itself over and over in his mind until he could hardly bear to be himself. It worried him because of his mother. It had never happened before with a place, but now he feared it was starting to happen even with that.

It was the house, of course, the big house. He kept seeing flashes of the house in his mind, like a series of broken photographs. The ivy, outside the glass door, its huge dark rich green leaves spreading over the gravel path and up the stone walls; the quiet space of lawn with a half circle of trees shaping it that was the further view. He tried to think what trees they were, but his mind was blank there, empty of photographs. He could see the furthest view of all, the little bridge over the ditch at the other side of the lawn, with the pine post sawn off at one end but not at the other. He wondered why that was. He could see that clearly, as he could the wire pulling away on the outside door.

And inside, the room they had broken into (he changed that quickly in his mind to 'went into') . . . After all, the door had been open. He could see the books on three walls, the pinkish-red curtain that seemed to match them, the honey-coloured floor boards. Even more clearly he could see the room upstairs where he had felt there was something wrong. What *was* it? And the dog – he tried not to see the dog at the top of the stairs. But the image persisted – its body half-flattened in terror but barking at them on and on until Pete had kicked it into a room.

A week and a day had gone past since the raid and he was still thinking about it, on and on, over and over. It was Saturday, with nothing to break up the time. He wheeled his old bike out of the shed. He always rode and rode when he was worried or upset. It tired and calmed him at the same time. But this time, crazily, he found that his bike was taking him wherever he could get a glimpse of the house.

He cycled up to Blackwood – just a usual route – but then he'd turned into Coromandel Parade and ridden down its winding length searching for the house. He caught glimpses of it but didn't stop for the road was too narrow. He cycled over Murray's Bridge and turned left, then down and into the back end of MacAlister. And there was his best view. He looked over the fields where cows still grazed even though new houses were going up everywhere, to the Institute Building with the pigeons on the roof and the big house beside it. He could see the spread of its roofs, the grove of peppermints where the others had waited, the slope of its canvas blinds, white and brown against the rich mellow brown of the stone.

'Hey, Gunno.'

He turned, still on the bike. It was Wally, his face wide with welcome.

'What 'ya doing, Gunno?'

'Nothing much.'

'You seen something?'

'Na.'

'Can you think of anything to do?'

'Nup.' Gunno tried to rouse himself. 'You could help me take some bottles to the Scouts.'

'Nup,' said Wally, disappointed. 'I don't feel like doing anything useful.'

'Well,' said Gunno, pedalling off. 'See you.'

'We could go skating at the Centre,' Wally called desperately as Gunno started to slide from view. 'I'll shout you.'

At the top of MacAlister Gunno looked back. Wally was still where he had left him – staring over the Vernons' fields. He'd be trying to see what Gunno had found so fascinating.

Gunno rode home. He'd been pretty sure the bottles idea would put Wally off. He didn't want to see anyone, least of all anyone from the gang. It was funny, he thought, how lately he always seemed to be bumping into Wally, or rather, Wally into him. He wanted, quite urgently, to finish that queer book he had picked up in the boy's room at the big house – about a dog, a nice enough dog originally, that went mad. He knew there was a reason for his feeling of urgency about reading it, but he didn't want to think about it now. But as the day wore on, the longest he could ever remember, he realised why he wanted to finish the book and why he especially didn't want to see anyone from the gang.

It was because he wanted to return the book; he wanted to go back. Yet he knew it was crazy to go back. It was certainly crazy to go back so soon. And if he did, he would be jeopardising the whole gang. I'll just put the book in the letter-box, he thought in a muddled sort of a way. It seemed very important to get it back somehow. But as Saturday turned painfully into Sunday he knew that the letter-box was not enough, stupid even, for it would draw attention to what would not have been missed. And what he really wanted was to get inside that house again. There was something there, something that was pulling him back.

He managed to achieve a certain amount of peace by thinking that he would go on Monday after school. That would give him two hours to get in and out before anyone came home. It was only then that he realised. Wally. He had talked about the man and the woman coming home 'every day in the one car – a white Renault 12 – at 6.28 sharp'. But not the boy. There had been no mention of a boy coming home. And yet there was his room. Perhaps he was on holiday, on exchange perhaps, like Sharon up the road. Ill in hospital. He'd better watch the house for a couple of afternoons to check that no one else *did* come home. He felt frustrated at the thought of having to wait, yet obviously he would have to. What he wanted to do was mad enough as it was: no need to make it madder. On Monday he would start watching.

He lay on his bed and looked out at the reserve. His was a pleasant room with a peaceful view. There were children on the swings and two up the giant oak tree, calling shrilly to one another in the distanced, unreal sort of way that you get through glass. His house was quiet and empty as usual. His father was always working. He pulled himself slowly from the bed and went to the fridge for a drink, glancing at his father's message for the day as he opened it:

Dear Gunno,
Back about 8. Will pick up a chicken.
Have a good day.
Love,
Dad.

Gunno reflected that he had two fathers – his Dad-on-the-fridge with his cheerful messages and his

Dad-home-from-work, fretful and too tired to want to do anything. Not that there was any money to do anything with. He could hardly say to his father, 'Been in a raid recently, Dad. Thought we might go out and celebrate'.

The money still lay thick at the bottom of his drawer – bank notes from the big house. He wondered what he could do with it.

It was after school on Wednesday. Gunno rode home almost at fever pitch. He let himself in, dropped his bag in the hall, and checked the fridge for messages. He'd watched both days and no one had come home till 6.28, just as Wally had said. He was always proud of his times, Wally. Not 'about 6.30' as the more slap-dash Pete would have said, or more cautious like Jess: 'It seems they always come home at the same time . . .' she would have begun, meaning that you can never quite rely on 'facts' like that. But to Wally it was fact: 'at 6.28 they come home', which made you feel certain that they would – let them dare otherwise.

He could have walked, but he felt safer having a bike, like a get-away car must seem to real robbers. He never thought of himself as that, as a thief, but rather as a member of a society, basically honourable, that dealt kindly with its clients. He left his bike leaning into an old hedge at the top of MacAlister, the dull green of its frame fading quietly into the leaves.

He walked in the back way past the apple orchard. There was no one around, just a splotchy white mare nibbling at the grass in the overgrown paddock next to the orchard. Even she hardly spared him a glance. He walked up the drive casually, as if it were his own place, and on up the brick path to the verandah. He pulled open the damaged outer door that he had pictured so clearly in his mind, and knocked. He could hear barking, but no one quietening it. He pictured the dog at the top of the stairs. He knocked again and the barking exploded into frantic yaps. He could hear the dog clumping down the stairs, and there was its head again, sticking out the cat door. And then it stopped: miraculously it stopped barking.

'Hi, fella,' said Gunno, amazed and rather touched by the effect he seemed to have on the dog.

He tried the handle, but it twisted back on itself again. Then round to the side door, so welcoming that last time. But of course it was locked too. Then he checked the windows on the lower level. I must be crazy, staying here, he thought at intervals, as he methodically looked for a catch that was loose, a screen that could be pulled back. *Rule 1: no damage to property*. That was a hard rule, but nevertheless one that they'd somehow managed to keep. He could imagine what Jess would say if she could see him, and how she would look – even taller, bigger than usual, scornful, her eyes hard as the green stones at the sea.

There was no way in at ground level. He knew he should give up now. And then he spotted it – an open window on the top storey. It was on the east side, the side that faced the road, but there were so many huge trees in the way, including an enormous ash. It wouldn't be so easy in winter, he thought, and then wondered why an unnecessary thought like that should crowd his mind. There was even an extension ladder, lightweight, aluminium, resting conveniently on the south side. He shifted it over slightly, so that it was well screened from the road, and swung himself on and up it. He took three steps across the roof, opened the window wider, and dropped silently inside.

He had landed in a bathroom, one with white tiles and green walls – cool-looking if a bit messy. There were circles of brown on the floor where old patches of water had dried in. Towels were hanging carelessly over rails and one was lying in a heap on the floor.

The bathroom led into a study, and there, facing him, was the dog, still not barking, just looking at him with its serious brown eyes.

'Hello,' he said cautiously. 'I've come to return a book.'

The dog's tail started to wag, slightly and slowly at first, and then more surely. There was something dreamlike about the whole thing, Gunno thought, giving himself a hard pinch. It hurt all right. But it was like some dreams he had where the sound track seemed to be switched off, where there was action and apparent conversation yet no sound. Dreams of his mother were often like this.

He patted the dog and it followed him as he tiptoed through to the bedroom where he had taken the money. The bed was unmade again he noticed. He went through the broad passageway to the room that seemed to draw him back the most. It was a lovely house, bigger than he had remembered. Without the gang in it and their noise it had become perfect.

The door was shut as he had somehow known it would be. There was something about a shut door, he thought, looking at it – exciting and menacing at the same time. He started to get a sort of sick feeling that when he opened the door there would be somebody there, waiting, or at any rate, there. Perhaps it would be the boy, lying on top of the red quilt, reading. He leant on the door, listening, then turned the handle slowly and stared into the widening space.

But there was no one there, only himself. It all looked exactly as he had left it almost a fortnight before. I'd better put the book back, he thought. After all, that was what he was supposed to have come for. Yet at the same time he felt a strange reluctance. Once he had done that, of course, he could go – and he didn't want to. But he did put it back, exactly where it had been before. And then he found that his hands were reaching for another one.

It was as he was selecting a book from this forbidden library that he realised what was wrong. There *was* something wrong with the room but it was nothing you could see, although it was a bit odd too how dusty the books were. He ran his finger down the spine of the one he was holding and looked at it. The lines on the pad of his finger were etched in black. That wasn't it though; that wasn't what he'd noticed and not noticed that first day. What was wrong with the room was its smell: the room smelt musty, unused, as if no one ever came into it.

Chapter Three

Gunno always liked it when the gang met at the beach. He often left early, to spend time there on his own. That was what he did on the Sunday after he had 'visited' (as he phrased it in his mind) the big house for the second time.

It was quiet on the roads and he had whizzed down Shepherd's Hill and was on Brighton Road and then at the jetty almost before he realised it. The sky was overcast – a sort of determined block white – and although the sun couldn't get through, it was suffusing the patch over the jetty with a yellowish stain. Gunno thought it looked like the weird sky in a painting where something ominous is about to happen.

He padlocked his bike to a stand south of the jetty and swung himself over the cement wall and onto the steps. The beach was hushed, also like a painting before the artist puts in the people, and the sand looked silvery and untouched and felt cool beneath his feet. Gunno could tell, though, from how close the air felt around him already and from the subdued menace of the sky that it wouldn't be long before the soft sand would be too hot to stand on. Now at the jetty he could see patches of people moving around slowly on the beach and in the sea – as if they were cold-blooded creatures that needed the sun to warm them.

He wandered nearer to the water. There were pools everywhere and inlets. In between these the sand was hard and sharply ribbed. He could feel the soles of his feet curving over it. He paddled in a pool, looking through the clear water at the perfect ribs of the sand. He was just starting to enjoy the empty free feeling that the beach always gave him when he was on his own, when he saw, bending over a pool closer to the sea, what looked very much like Jess: big-boned, long-legged in emerald bathers. They would match her eyes, if it were she, when she turned round.

He glanced impatiently at his watch. It was still early. She shouldn't be here yet. He walked slowly nearer, reluctantly at first, and stood behind her. She was poking around in some light green and pinkish traces of seaweed with a stick that she had found. A passing dog looked interested in it. She turned round with the half-pace movements of the other people on the beach and gave him her sudden smile.

'It's early,' she said, almost as a question. Then perhaps thinking that if it were a question it would apply equally to her, she added: 'I came ...' then stopped again, as if she didn't know how to go on.

'Early to be alone,' Gunno completed it for her. He laughed. 'I know, I did too. Well, there's plenty of room to be alone.' He pointed to the sweep of sand curving around the vast bay.

But she didn't move. 'I don't mind being alone with you,' she said; then realising how it might sound, 'I mean, I don't mind being alone together.'

They both laughed at that, though Gunno thought that he probably did mind: without the shelter of the gang, being with Jess was something different, something he wasn't sure he wanted, especially just now. It was hard to hide things from Jess.

They wandered up the beach in a wavering line, from pool to pool, from inlet to inlet. Gunno waded in every pool and sat down in one – the water was so warm and clear close to shore. Further out it looked a dull rather murky green for the sky was still overcast and the light subdued.

'You don't have to be yourself at the beach,' Jess said, as they walked on. 'You could be anyone. That's what I like about it.'

'Anonymous,' said Gunno. 'The beach and the sea and the sky make us anonymous.'

'At home,' Jess pursued, ignoring his wording, 'you have to be too much yourself. Or at least the self that everyone thinks you are. Here, you could be anyone.'

'You seem like you to me,' said Gunno, but knew that she was probably thinking of her small brothers. She had three of these and as the only girl, and much older at that, she was expected to help a lot. 'The dogs seem the same,' he added, looking at a couple that were belting past, tongues well out. 'Maybe just a bit more the same than usual.'

'I'd like a dog,' said Jess. 'I've always wanted a dog.'

'You'd have the money,' Gunno suggested, 'to buy most kinds of dog.'

'But you can't say that,' said Jess. 'You can't say you have the money to buy and feed it, even if you have. Then it's "But where . . .? But how . . .?" Anyway, it's not just that. Mum says there's enough mess. Dogs mean hairs and dirty feeding bowls to her.'

'I know what you mean about the money,' said Gunno. 'I've run into the same problem. I've never had a dog either,' he added. He thought of the dog at the big house. He wondered again why it liked him so much, why it trusted him. Funny sort of watch dog, he thought, but affectionately, as he got quite a detailed flash of its long face, pointy ears like a fox and neat, fresh-looking white paws.

Gunno felt that he had better change his thoughts quickly before Jess looked into his mind and saw the little dog sitting there. But it was already too late.

'Penny for them,' said Jess, scrutinising his face. 'Or how many cents should it be?'

'Five maybe,' said Gunno, 'but it doesn't sound the same. I was just thinking,' he lied slightly, 'that the dogs are starting to go off the beach. Look, all the good ones on leads are disappearing and the bad ones are beginning to feel insecure.'

'That means it's time for Pete and Wally,' said Jess.

Gunno had an image of them then, thundering down Jetty Road, racing one another to the beach, flinging their bikes down anywhere and diving off the deep end of the jetty. There would be a flash of blond hair and tanned bodies in bright blue satiny bathers, Wally's a bit less bright than Pete's, and then, as you searched the water, the gleam of white teeth grinning at you. It wouldn't be peaceful when they came.

'They'll be racing down Brighton Road by now,' said Gunno with a bit of a sigh. 'Putting on a last minute spurt.'

Jess turned to him and gave her chuckly laugh. 'An end to peace,' she said.

Gunno wondered what the business of the day would be. It seemed too good a day for business. And it seemed much too soon to be planning another raid. He hadn't managed yet to spend any of what he had, though he would go into town and buy some books. He looked forward to that. But he knew better than to ask Jess why they were meeting. That was another of Jess's rules: gang business was only ever discussed when they were all there together.

In the distance he could see Pete and Wally at the jetty, leaping off their bikes. And as if at a signal, the whole beach seemed to explode into proper movement and colour and chaos. Multi-coloured umbrellas were going up – tilting at the sun; beach towels were being spread out; children were running everywhere.

Even the sky was changing. The cloud was breaking up with frail wisps of blue appearing. The water was taking on a hard gleam. Jess sighed as they walked back, faces to the sun, looking at the busy cars lining up along the esplanade. A child threw bread in front of them.

'Look,' said Gunno, 'look at that one.' A seagull with one red leg hopped in a business-like way on the sand, then launched itself into the air.

'He got it first,' said Jess, amazed. But at the same moment she saw the flash of blue bathers that was Pete, and the more muted flash that was Wally. They were diving off the jetty.

Chapter Four

Gunno was pottering around in the big house. There was no other way to put it. It was ridiculous really, but he felt as if he had lived in the house or at least known of it, all his life. He was taking quite a housewifely interest, he realised, amused at himself, as he walked around from room to room with the dog at his heels.

He was filled with strange longings: to make the bed, for instance, or tidy up in the kitchen. Particularly strange, considering he never wanted to do these things at home. Here the dishes were piled up in the sink and the margarine and even the milk had been left out of the fridge. Either the people had to leave very early in the morning or they weren't very good at getting up. Everywhere there was the sign of haste: the wardrobe door in the bedroom left open on what seemed to Gunno endless clothes, the shoe polish lying with its lid off on top of the washing machine. It was turning hard and cracked already. He just wished he could straighten things up.

He wandered restlessly out of the kitchen and into the built-in part of the verandah outside it. Leafy pot plants and one with white flowers, in shapes that suggested movement, were languishing in the heat. He filled a jam jar at the laundry tap and watered the flowering one. But he stopped at that: they wouldn't notice if he just watered one, people as neglectful as they were. And after some thought he put the milk away in the fridge. It was too much to leave it out.

He wondered then if his interest might be to do with his having a key – he'd found a spare key conveniently marked 'Geoff Lethbridge, Back Door' hanging up in the kitchen. He'd taken it and had it copied at the local shoe repairer's. Then he'd let himself in – just as though he were the boy of the house. Maybe that was why he was feeling responsible, for the milk, for the plant, for the unmade bed. It was becoming his house.

He thought then about the boy's room, where the bed was always made. He wondered if he should open a window to get rid of the smell and he even climbed the stairs to do so, the dog still following him faithfully. But he got the same sick feeling when he looked at the shut door, and the same tightening around his heart as he opened it. But the room was empty of boys. What was most noticeable, now that he had identified it, was the musty smell. But he decided not to open the window: that was just the sort of change that anyone, even the least observant, would notice. Besides, he was getting used to it and it gave him a safe feeling: it meant that nobody came into the room except himself. Nothing was disturbed. It was like being in his own place.

It was strange having your own place in someone else's house; strange too that the room was in their house and they never went into it. He walked over to the bed and picked up the book that was lying on the small table beside it. *A Wizard of Earthsea*. Idly he turned over the pages, read the dust jacket and the opening paragraph. He turned back to the fly-leaf. There was writing on it:

To Hugh,
With all our love,
Mum and Dad
Christmas 1986.

He felt a rising excitement, as if he had found a clue. Well, he had, of course he had. He lay down on top of Hugh's red bedcover and turned to the beginning. He read several chapters, very quickly, then put the book back on the table. It seemed right for someone of his age. That meant Hugh was about fourteen or fifteen now, if he was twelve, thirteen in 1986. He started to lose a bit of interest in him then – he had thought that Hugh was the same age he was – and he couldn't be, he was older.

But he didn't lose interest in the book. It spoke to him more clearly than anything he had ever read. Yet it was a fantasy, set in a mythic land no one would ever hear of or travel to – and it was about a boy with magic powers. When the boy had only been a small child he had saved his village from its enemy by causing a fog to fall and blanket all the houses in it.

Gunno reflected on what he had read with a growing excitement, and his thoughts swung back and encompassed Hugh in them, for the book had been lying beside Hugh's bed. It must have been the last thing he had read before he'd gone off or else the first thing his mother would expect him to want to read when he got back. What he particularly liked was how no one, not even the boy's father, questioned that the boy had such power. No one put it down just to coincidence or luck that the child had worked a spell and the fog had fallen. He thought of the boy earlier, raging at his own weakness. 'There was power in him, if he knew how to use it.' He said the words over to himself, more than once.

He glanced at his watch. The time went quickly here, not dragging as it did at home. That was strange because he was just as alone here. But was he? He looked around the room, at the objects which already seemed so familiar to him. He liked the bed too, better than his own at home. It felt firmer, harder. And then there was the dog, lying on the floor beside him. He leant over and scratched behind its ears. It was funny, the things in this room – the books, the models, the furniture – seemed not just more familiar but more nearly his own than the objects at home. Of course that was always the trouble with a rented place: it never seemed truly yours, never seemed really home even when you put your own things in it. He remembered how Jess had reacted when she'd asked him about his house.

She'd ridden home from school with him one day. 'Nice place you've got,' she said.

'Not bad,' he said, but without any sense of pride. 'It's not ours; we're renting.'

'Renting,' she repeated. And then, 'Suppose you'll have your own place soon.'

But Gunno had explained that wasn't likely. Even though his father had two jobs so that he hardly saw him, neither of them paid much. And then there was Mum.

Jess had seemed pleased but as if she were trying to hide it, whether because his father was out so much or because they were fairly poor he hadn't been sure at the time. Probably on both counts, he thought now, for it was shortly after this that she invited him to join the gang. She'd obviously decided he could do with the money.

That was what they'd talked about at the beach the other day when Pete and Wally had come. They'd decided not to do another raid for a few weeks because they all had plenty of money still. Indeed the common problem seemed to be how to get rid of it safely. Wally was the most ambitious – he wanted to buy a new skate board with his, perhaps hoping unconsciously to shake free of his hand-me-down image, Gunno thought. Pete rightly pointed out that their mother would ask questions – and their father, if it occurred to him.

'I could put a dent in it,' Wally had said.

They all stared at him. 'A dent,' they echoed.

'Yeah. Then she'll just think it's a second-hand one I picked up.'

'It *will* be a second-hand one,' said Gunno, 'if you put a dent in it.'

'Of all the dumb ideas,' said Pete fiercely.

'There's no point in getting all heated up about a skate board that doesn't exist,' Jess had said, trying to calm them all down. 'It *is* a problem, though. I've seen a painting I like, but how can I get that?'

'A *painting*!' Pete was appalled. 'What's it of?'

'Oh, trees, bushes, paths, stuff like that,' said Jess vaguely.

'No one knows how much paintings are worth anyway,' said Gunno. 'Just say you picked it up second-hand for the frame.'

Jess considered this in a pleased way, staring at Gunno with her green eyes. 'What do *you* spend your money on, Gunno?' she'd asked suddenly, as if it had just occurred to her that she had no idea what he'd spend it on and hence no idea really of what he was like.

'Mostly I don't,' he said. He wasn't going to confess to buying books with it. Nobody else read in the gang.

'What do you save it up for then?' she pursued.

But Pete broke in there, bored by any talk that didn't centre upon himself. 'You want to buy things you can use up. That's best. Easy to hide. Cigarettes, lottery tickets for Porsches, and go to the pictures, ice skating, Pizza Hut, that kind of thing.'

'That makes sense in a way,' said Gunno. 'But then you still haven't got anything after, have you?'

'Like what?' said Pete, aggressively.

'Like a skate board,' said Wally, as the conversation came full circle.

Looking round Hugh's room Gunno sympathised with Wally. He could see it must be nice to own things. He'd never thought about it before, but he'd like to own or at least belong to this house. He glanced at the little dog who was still lying patiently on the floor beside the bed licking her white paws. It'd even be nice to own the little dog: to say, 'This is my dog,' with just that inflection in your voice. Not that he imagined you ever could own anything in the sense of its being yours, unchanged, relating only to you, for ever. The dog, any dog, would die, the house might burn down or be bulldozed. He'd learnt that lesson early, when his mum had gone away. Nothing was for ever.

Chapter Five

It was the following week. Gunno patted the dog abstractedly. He was feeling annoyed with the woman who lived in the house – Hugh's mother, Geoff's wife, the dog's mistress. She was so untidy. She owned a big house with plenty of cupboards and drawers to store things in yet the place always looked a mess. It wasn't only that the dishes were piled up in the sink every day that he'd been here, and that the bed was unmade. It was her study as well.

It should have been perfect with picture windows on two sides that brought the garden right into the room, but it wasn't. He looked around. There was an enormous black desk with a white telephone, a yellow lamp that bent and swivelled, and a very capable-looking big cream office typewriter, not to mention the luxury black-and-white padded typing chair, the comfortable brown one and the large electric fire, waiting for winter. Yet you could hardly see an inch of her desk for books, papers, folders, paper-clips, tissues. Some of the books were even lying open. He picked up the top one – 'Anne Lethbridge', it said, in sprawling writing. Right, then. Anne. He was feeling annoyed with Anne.

He had thought all women were like Jess and like his mother – neat, methodical. He could have shaken Anne. He could hardly tidy up her desk, he thought, looking at the mess of it, yet his fingers ached to do so. Perhaps he could just do a little. He rearranged her folders and smoothed her papers until the edges were straight. The pile of books on her desk looked as if it would topple. He pulled it straight too. Now he could see strips of the black desk. If only he could do a thorough job, but he daren't. It was like the pot plants all over again – he looked after the plant where the flowers uncurled like ballet dancers but that was all. It hurt him though to see the leafy plants beside it droop and turn yellow-green.

His interest had spread now from the house to the garden. Yet again he daren't spend time in it. Every day he just quickly patted the black bunny – it was turning steadily browner in the warm spring sun – and let himself in with his key. On a sunny day like this one he walked restlessly from room to room looking out at the various parts of the garden. But the view from Anne's study was the best, the widest of all. From it you could see the whole garden on the south and west sides.

But looking at a garden wasn't the same as being in it. Inside he couldn't smell the lemon-scented gums after rain or hear the birds. The garden was full of them. He had seen rainbow lorikeets, Adelaide rosellas, magpies, willy wagtails and honey-eaters. There was a wattlebird now at the window – hopping, really hopping, both legs tightly together, from branch to branch of the plum tree. It had two pink patches on its cheeks as if someone had stuck confetti on them.

He would love to spend time in the garden with the birds and the rabbit. There was a hammock too – a yellow string one cradled between two trees in the pittosporum grove. He went into Hugh's room to see if he could spot it from there – but the view was cut off.

His mind reverted to Anne. She didn't even bother to keep her son's room nice for him coming home. She didn't dust or even air it. It had the smell of a museum. 'With all our love, Hugh,' it said in the books in the sprawling writing he knew now was hers, but she didn't look after his things. He had looked through Hugh's books and found others that had been given as presents – 'Christmas 1984' for example, 'For your birthday, 2/2/82'. The dates and the choice of book seemed to support his view that Hugh, wherever he was (probably run away to escape the clutter, he thought sourly), must be two or three years older than Gunno was now.

There was something strange about one of the presents, though. It had been *A Wizard of Earthsea* that he had found lying by Hugh's bed, and the date in that, Christmas 1986. That was all right. But then he'd found the sequels to it, *The Tombs of Atuan* and *The Farthest Shore* done up in plastic wrapping at the back of a shelf with a birthday card still attached to them:

To Hugh,
With all our love, (the usual style)
from Mum and Dad
2/2/87.

He'd opened *The Tombs* and found that some of the pages were stuck together. Hugh had never read it then, even though *A Wizard of Earthsea*, that he'd got only the Christmas before, already had the used look that suggested more than one reading. There were no later inscriptions in any of the books – no wonder – no wonder they'd never given him a book again as a present. Perhaps they'd switched to models. He examined the ones high up on the wall. Yet they looked quite old.

He moved back to Anne's study as the brightest room in the house. Idly he looked through the pile of books he had rearranged on Anne's desk. She seemed to be keen on poetry – there were quite a few books of poems. He opened one of them at a marker. He stared at the words:

Ere my heart beats too coldly and faintly
To remember sad things, yet be gay,
I would sing a brief song of the world's little children
Magic hath stolen away.

The primroses scattered by April,
The stars of the wide Milky Way,
Cannot outnumber the hosts of the children
Magic hath stolen away.

There were more verses but he shut the book. The poem disturbed him.

'Gunno,' his father said that night. 'I've had a letter from your mother.'

'Oh yes.' Gunno's voice was deliberately casual. He'd brought the letter from the box and knew the writing and the postmark.

'She wants you to write to her, son.'

'I do. I have.'

'Yes, but she's disappointed in your letters. She says they're ... Now, what was the word she used?' He searched through the letter. '"Perfunctory", that was it. She means ...'

'I know what she means.'

'She means that you never really tell her anything, not anything important.'

'Maybe there's nothing important to tell.'

His father looked at him sharply, and seemed about to say something, then decided against it. 'Perhaps not,' was all that he said. 'Still, I think you could try more.

She says . . .' He broke off here, sounding a bit embarrassed. 'You know how fanciful she is,' he went on, preparing him. 'She says she feels like a plant that hasn't been watered.'

Instantly Gunno saw Anne's pine bench with its plants, one of them flowering bravely amidst the fading leaves.

'Just tell me you'll try.'

Gunno looked at his father, but his mind had already slid away – back to his house, to his garden. 'I'll think about it,' he said cautiously, but his grey eyes were cold. 'I'll think about trying.'

What he was really thinking about was the book on Anne's desk – the book of poems. What *had* that poem been called? 'The Truants', that was it. It was a strange poem – sad but somehow triumphant – it had an edge of triumph to it. 'Magic hath stolen away'. He said it over to himself. And the title: how did that fit in? It was only when he was in bed that night that he realised what the poem had made him think of – or rather, *who* it made him think of. The poem made him think of Hugh.

Chapter Six

Gunno's hand was actually trembling as he turned the lock and let himself out of the rented house. It wasn't quite nine o'clock yet, but he couldn't make himself wait any longer. Most of the school crowd should have gone by now.

He'd decided to spend the whole day at the big house – skip school for it. What he would be able to fit into a day! He enjoyed his snippets of time there, but a whole day! And it was perfect weather – cool, sunny. The house would be at its best with the sun streaming through the door of the dining-room by late morning.

He rode the long way round Rokeby Crescent, to take up a bit more time, wobbling on his bike as he climbed up to the graveyard – he wished they didn't spell it 'Cemetary'. And it was then, just as he was passing the sign, that he got the strangest feeling that someone was following him. He'd heard something or seen a flash of movement, yet when he turned there was nothing – no one was there. He got off his bike and stared into the long grass between the graves. Plenty of places to hide: the gang had hidden there themselves once. He waited a moment, then shot off down the steep slope of Dune Avenue.

He took the bike path above the main road but then hid under a large olive bush. There seemed to be nothing unusual. Someone was mowing the grass, there was a steady stream of cars up the main road, a woman was walking her dog. He wondered if Sam (for that was what he called the dog at the big house when he gave her a name) ever came for a walk this way.

He waited for ten minutes, timing it carefully on his watch as if it were important, then did a detour round Rokeby Crescent, from the entrance almost opposite the big house. He rode into the park and sat under the oak tree. The place was deserted at this time in the morning. He pulled out his latest borrowing from the house and pretended to read. It was *Swallows and Amazons*, a Christmas present to Hugh in 1984. It was just the sort of book he would have carried around with him when he was ten. Just the sort of book he was carrying around with him now, he thought with a smile.

Sometimes Gunno felt he was trying to catch up on Hugh's childhood, and through it, his own, by reading his books: books like *The Stone Doll of Sister Brute, The Borrowers, A Swarm in May, Ash Road*. And always, in among this other reading, *A Wizard of Earthsea*. He hadn't read all that much since his mother had left. She had been the one who had always read to him, and been interested in what he read for himself. It had been the old sagas she had read to him mainly – especially one: that one she had read to him over and over. But because she had, that was the one he had tried to block completely from his mind.

He climbed the oak tree and stared out between its branches – still nothing. Perhaps he had imagined it. He always felt jumpy before he got to the big house and then so much at peace when he was there. And today was meant to be special. He climbed down, picked up his bike, and went on his original route past the graveyard. He looked at his watch. Blast! He'd lost half an hour already of his precious whole day.

He let himself in the door thankfully and called to the little dog. She hardly barked at all now, and stopped as soon as he appeared on the verandah. Her wide body melted against his leg as he bent to pat her.

Gunno eased himself into Geoffrey's armchair. The pink television pages had been well marked at the weekend, and Geoffrey had run off another video. Gunno got up and looked indulgently at the new label on the tape that was lying on the TV table. Well, perhaps he could get interested in that himself. A Swedish play about a milk stand. Sounded a bit strange. He slid it into the recorder and settled down comfortably to watch the film. He glanced at his watch. They would all be doing double maths at school now. He adjusted the volume and sat waiting, in a pleased way, to be entertained. The dog stretched out at his feet.

It *had* just been about a milk stand. This man wouldn't put his milk cans where the other people in the town now had to – it had all been centralised. And someone, either from the government, or certainly with their approval, came and knocked his milk stand down, breaking it up with a big truck. Then he built another one, and another one. Always the same thing happened. His neighbours tried to reason with him. 'You're foolish,' they said. 'Give in, do what we do.' But he wouldn't. He said if you give in on one thing you end up having to give in on everything.

His wife supported him. They took turns sitting on the milk stand, guarding it. The man who collected the milk was amused. He began to stop for their lone milk churn, and they'd give him a cup of coffee.

But finally the truck that was used to destroy the milk stand came in the night. It was freezing, snowing, with big drifts that the truck had first to shift off the road, but the man kept sitting there, so cold on his stand. The truck had come closer and closer but he wouldn't get off; he sat, small, modest-looking yet so defiant, and in the end the truck gave up and went away.

Then the neighbours and the further community started to take sides. The fiancée of the man who kept knocking the milk stand down said she didn't want to have any more to do with him if that was the sort of man he was. And the neighbours came in the night and built him a special, elaborate milk stand when he and his wife got forcibly removed from the old one and it got knocked down yet again. The one that the neighbours built looked like a little church – in an arch shape – with two seats in it for them to sit in.

This was so touching in the play that it made Gunno's eyes film over. Until then he had thought he was looking at it to see what Geoffrey was like – what he watched – but now he was pulled into the play himself. But really he'd been pulled in from the moment the man's difficulties had become greater, when there was no wood around for him to build more milk stands and he had to go out and buy some. But even then, eventually people started to supply him with fresh wood. Each time they made the stand with stronger and stronger timber, but in the end it still got knocked down. Until one night all the neighbours came to help. They built the stand out of cement, let it harden and then cloaked it in a wooden stand. Then they all settled back to watch for the truck to come . . .

Gunno sat up and blinked. He liked stories, maybe because he'd had so many read to him when he'd been little. He'd loved that Swedish film. He was amazed that it had been built out of so little – not like the soapies he often watched at home – just the idea of the stand and the man's persistence. The rest had been elaboration. Maybe persistence was more important than anything. He would like to feel as persistent as that about something. Persistence is when you keep on with something when everything, everyone including yourself, is screaming at you to stop. He wondered what the difference was between being persistent and being obsessive. What if the man had lost?

He went up to Anne's study, the little dog trotting happily after him. He looked at Anne's pile of books, dangerously angled again. Her journal was lying on the top. It was a corded book in beige with buttery-yellow end-papers. It was a mild restful colour which he somehow associated with the house. He thought of things as colours. School was grey and black, home was dull blue, this house was a variety of cool greens and this soft yellow of the book. He knew it was her journal because he had glanced at it quickly once before, then shut it just as quickly. He could hardly read her diary even if he would like to know more about her.

He looked at the clutter on her desk. He felt a kind of reluctant affection for her as he stared into the murkiness of her latest cup of coffee. If only she'd remember to stick the cup on a mat – it'd be leaving a ring on the lino. He looked quickly away from the dead flies that he could see dotting the window sill. No, that was too much. Gunno took a bit of paper from the bathroom and flushed them down the toilet. He was sure she wouldn't notice that. He must remember to check though that he'd taken the video out. Now that he was using more things in the house he had to be much more careful. It would be so easy to leave something out of place in a way that people would recognise they wouldn't have done themselves.

He'd forgotten to bring his drink bottle, as he'd meant to do, and he was parched. He'd go downstairs in a minute. He knew he shouldn't really sit in the study. These big picture windows worked both ways, of course. Just last week he'd had a feeling that someone was watching him. Certainly anyone passing down the drive could easily see him sitting here. Yet the risk added to his delight in the study – and on a mild day it was the nicest room in the house, despite the mess. On even a warm day it was already too hot. Then Gunno moved into the boy's room to read, or sat at his desk to write in the journal he'd started for himself.

He was so thirsty that he would just have to help himself to something out of the fridge. He couldn't stand the tap water. He ran downstairs. There was only milk, but that would do. Good. Two cartons were already opened. If he just took a bit from each, no one would ever know.

He had such a feeling of well-being that he poured himself a whole glass of milk – almost till it overflowed. Skimmed milk, but never mind; it still tasted good when you were thirsty and hungry. He drank it from his favourite glass – an odd-shaped thickish glass with a definite green tinge to it. He loved green glass: it reminded him of the sea. It reminded him too of Jess.

The dog was still at his feet, delighted to have company, especially his, it seemed. 'Well, boy,' he said to her (all dogs were males to him), looking around for something to bring her within the circle of well-being too. 'What about a nice brush and comb?'

The dog looked up at him eagerly, her tail starting to wag. Gunno squatted beside her, gently brushing and trying to disentangle the matted bits in her fur. She had burs on her legs too. She licked him gratefully as he got rid of them, holding on to her hair close to her skin so that it wouldn't hurt when he pulled them out. Later he tried combing, but she snapped at him a couple of times when the comb pulled on her skin, and he was content to go back to brushing.

He wondered if it had been Hugh who had looked after her. And thinking of Hugh, he wondered with growing disquiet what had happened to him. All letters and cards Anne pinned untidily across the board in the kitchen and left them there, till they yellowed and their corners turned. But, although he always checked, there had never been a letter, never a card even, from Hugh.

The little dog looked lovely when he had finished and seemed to be proud of herself. She stuck her chest out, its thick soft silvery hair matching her impeccable feet. 'What a pretty dog!' he said, giving her a brisk pat on the bottom so that she would know he had finished. She went off with playful little darts and skids, and came back like a miniature prancing horse, hardly touching the floor with her silky feet, with her yellow soft ball in her mouth.

Gunno pretended to groan, then he settled down to ten minutes of throwing the ball for her up the sixteen steps to the spare room above. Sometimes she collapsed on the top step, chewing at the ball, and he would go away, tired of waiting, but as soon as he had disappeared into the kitchen she let it go and he would hear it going plong, plong, plonkitty plong down the stairs. Then he would picture her sharp little foxlike face, head on the side watching it go, and he wouldn't be able to resist and back he would go to the bottom of the stairs and the same thing would happen all over again. I'm not going to let it go *this* easily, she seemed to say each time, although he tried to explain that it just wasn't in the rules to hold on to the ball and keep munching it when it finally came your way.

She never seemed to tire of this game, but Gunno did and he slid tactfully away from it. He thought: if only she could talk, if only she could tell him where Hugh had gone or even what he had been like. He often felt the little dog's disappointment when he walked away. How often had Hugh sent the ball up the stairs before he too grew tired of it and went away?

He walked up the stairs, trying not to look at the little dog sitting pensively at the top of them, her paws over the edge, and opened the door of the shut room cautiously, as he always did, as if this time there might be something, somebody there, waiting for him. But of course there was nothing.

Wherever Hugh was now, his mother didn't seem to have disturbed anything that was his. There were a number of dog-eared exercise books with torn blue covers piled high in one corner, in one of the leaning towers he was used to seeing in Anne's room. He picked up the top one and thumbed idly through it. It seemed to be Hugh's writing book.

It was just the usual scrawly look of the usual school exercise book. Maybe more scrawly than some. Even his margins were a mess, done in red, with the biro slipping off the ruler and making little trails and pathways away from the main line. And then there was his spelling. His spelling was awful! Gunno shuddered as he looked at it: not just the usual kind of mistakes that everybody makes – 'occured', 'cemetary', 'existance', but awful ones. 'Cryed', for example, 'freind', 'recieve'. A spectacularly bad speller then: not just ordinarily bad. And not even consistent.

Gunno turned over more pages. Hugh seemed to have a lot of pieces of writing started but not finished off. Gunno looked at some of his openings:

SHOPPING
(the usual exciting sort of heading)

Mum always used to shop on Fridays. When I was litel (really!). *I remember going shoping with Mum. We must have gone almost at the time when the shops were shuting, and we used to run everywehre, and in winter the lights were already on.*

Although I was so litle, I supose becuase somtimes it was so late, she got me to go for the veg while she got the meat, that sort of thing. I got into trouble once for getting fruit instead of veg, and we went home with what Mum thought was a big bag of potatos but was realy pears.

The essay petered out there. Gunno sighed. What could Anne expect sending a pre-schooler to get the shopping? And going at the last minute. It didn't really look as though Anne had changed.

He flicked through the rest of the pages with worn topics like *My Holidays, What I did on the long weekend,* and paused at a very short one which had aborted itself even sooner than most of the others:

AN ADVENTURE

I think it's too dificilt to have an adventure these days, at least if your with somone else. The only way maybe to have an adventure is to go some place on your own. Some place that nobody knows about.

Gunno didn't quite know why he was attracted to that one. Maybe it was just that it was so short. He read it again. He wondered what sort of place Hugh had had in mind. *Some place that nobody knows about.* Maybe he hadn't had any particular place in mind. And yet the piece sounded somehow as if he were thinking aloud, as if he were thinking of trying to have an adventure, some place on his own. But it didn't make sense, did it? Why should it be more of an adventure just because you were on your own? Yet maybe again he was right. If you went to the graveyard at night, say with Wally, it would just be fun. Then again, if you went by yourself it might well turn into something other. Or if he could have gone to the cemetery with Hugh . . . One thing sure about that, even if it had been possible, there would have been no point in drawing Hugh's attention to the spelling of the sign.

Chapter Seven

Gunno didn't really want to go to the meeting of the gang the next day. He wanted to be free to think his own thoughts: to think about the house, to think about Hugh. And when he got there he found that it was hard to keep his mind on the details, or really on anything actual at all.

Jess wasn't finding it hard, however. 'Let's do Ross Road next,' she said, sounding definite, sounding positive. 'It's steepish but private. Lots of trees. Big front gardens. Quiet.'

Gunno was drawing in the sand. He was trying to shape a wattlebird. He would search later for a thread of pink seaweed to make the confetti effect he had noticed on its cheeks.

He kept thinking about *A Wizard of Earthsea*, about the importance of naming in it. He liked the idea that people had a 'use' name and a 'true' name. The use name was the one that people used to name you; but your true name was something kept hidden. If people knew your true name then they had power over you.

That seemed right to Gunno. He always felt diminished somehow, almost enslaved, when someone asked him his name, rather than him offering it. It was true:

knowing someone's name gave you power over them. He was glad that no one, hardly anyone, knew his real name. His father, of course, knew it but never used it: his mother always used it, kept reading him that story, but now she was never there. He pulled the curtains of his mind across it, across her, as he always did. Sparrowhawk was the wizard's use name: but his true name was Ged.

'Gunno?' said Jess, a bit sharply.

He knew she would be thinking he was getting dreamier – a lot dreamier, she would think, if she could see the glazed look in his eyes. He kept looking down.

'What?' he said.

'Ross Road?'

'What about it?'

'For our next raid.'

'Oh, fine. Fine.' He tried to rouse himself. 'There are old houses there,' he contributed.

'And new places,' said Pete. 'It's a bit of a mixture.'

'What do you think, Wal?' asked Jess.

'Be a packet there,' said Wally. 'Might be risky. There's a house with an old lady – she's always in the garden.'

'We'll pick a cold day,' said Jess, 'if we can. Which house is it?'

'Second from the top.'

Gunno started drawing up the plan, blacking out the danger house first. 'We'd better skip the houses each side.'

'Seems a pity,' said Pete. 'Next door there's that two-storeyed one with the balconies.'

'Mm,' agreed Jess. 'Does seem a pity.'

'Yeah,' said Wally. 'Let's do that one. We'll be extra careful.'

Gunno looked glum. 'That's what we always seem to be saying these days, "We'll be extra careful". What that really means is that we're taking risks.'

'Unacceptable ones,' said Pete smugly, remembering what Gunno had said at an earlier meeting.

'Yes,' said Gunno, but not rising to the bait. 'It's only an ordinary precaution to skip the houses both sides of a house that looks risky. You all know that.' He looked pleadingly at Jess.

'It's just that the balcony one looks extra good, Gunno.' Jess spoke placatingly. 'But you're right, of course – we'll have to be very careful. Pete, Wally, do a really thorough check on the whole street. Let's take our time over this one.'

'We might go up and down putting pamphlets in boxes, if we can get hold of some,' said Wally. 'That would give us a chance to have a good look round.'

Gunno had gone back to sketching in his bird in the sand.

'Gunno isn't interested any more,' said Pete. 'His mind's on higher things, get it, like birds. Real ones,' he added, for Wally was starting to snigger. 'The other sort he doesn't notice.'

'Oh lay off, Pete,' said Gunno, looking bored, almost as if the gang banter were getting a bit beneath him. Once he would have laughed too.

'Gunno,' said Jess. 'What's wrong?' She stared out beyond the sand-bar to where Pete was trying to duck Wally.

'Wrong? Nothing. What should there be?' He was making channels in the wet sand with a stick. He could feel his mood lying heavy on her like the overcast sky. He looked around him. 'There's that one-legged seagull again. Reckon it's the same one?'

'Maybe,' said Jess. 'But you're just making an effort, aren't you? You couldn't really care less about the gull.'

'Making an effort?' he asked, echoing all her words now like an idiot.

'To be normal.'

'I thought I was normal,' said Gunno, looking at her for the first time.

Jess responded to the anxious look in his eyes. He could see she knew he was thinking about his mother.

'Normal to what you usually are, I mean.'

'What's that like?' he asked, as if he really wanted to please and be that for her.

'Well,' she said carefully, trying to answer seriously, 'you're always quiet, but you're happy quiet, if you know what I mean. Restful to be with. Now you're quiet, but it's as if you're about to explode. What *is* it, Gunno?'

Gunno sighed and looked out to sea. Pete and Wally were just little blobs in the ocean from here. He supposed they must be the same to them.

'I guess I'm just a bit tired,' he said.

'Tired? What's making you tired?'

He knew she was getting angry – no, upset was more the word. She was getting upset because he had moved away, moved away inside himself, somewhere she could no longer reach him. Perhaps he should try to tell her – try to tell her something. Not the truth, but something that would suggest the truth.

'I've got a sort of job after school,' he might say.

And *she* would say, 'Well, why didn't you say so? We'd have understood that. Why didn't you say?'

And Gunno would look at her, flushing. It wasn't the sort of job you could explain. 'I look after the dog,' he could have said. 'She gets lonely and bored shut up in the big house all day. I play with her – sometimes with the red, sometimes with the yellow soft ball. Then there's the pot plants, and the little bit of tidying I manage to do. Then there's filling out my journal and writing summaries of the books that I read. Then I watch Geoff's videos because I want to know more about what kind of people live there and I won't ever be able to meet them. Then,' (here he would hesitate, not quite wanting to formulate it, not even to himself), 'there's this problem about the boy.'

But of course, he couldn't say any of that.

'Well?' She was still waiting.

'Oh nothing. Nothing's wrong. Really.' He stood up and smiled down at her. He stretched out his hand. 'Come on, Jess. Let's have a swim.'

He could see that they were about to get very wet anyway. Pete and Wally were running towards them out of the sea, great sheets of water falling from them.

Chapter Eight

Gunno shut the book and walked over to the window. He stared sightlessly, disturbed by what he had read, at the swaying restless trees, at the moving colours that blew across the window in reflection as well. This had been more than Hugh usually wrote – he'd got further into this one, but no one seemed to have marked it. It was empty of red pen, except for the left-hand margin, dithering about as it usually did, uncertain of where to go. He turned and walked out of the room, shutting the door behind him. He would go downstairs and play Geoffrey's tape. The little dog trotted after him.

He switched on the recorder so that it would play in the lounge and settled back in Geoffrey's own comfortable grey-and-white wool armchair. He could tell it was Geoff's because it was often left in a position that suggested someone had been adjusting the video from it. Also there were scrape marks on the wooden floor where he had carelessly moved the chair – with himself inside it, Gunno suspected.

It was the tape of the first movement of a symphony, Brahms's second, but with someone explaining and introducing it. Whereas before when Gunno had heard music like this he had let it flow over him, not paying any particular attention to it, now he listened. He'd been used to thinking of music as a background: music in the shops, music in the doctor's waiting-room, pleasant maybe or unpleasant, according to other associations, but hardly ever attended to.

But this was different. The speaker was so enthusiastic and took you with him with such small steps that he made you attend. And gradually, as he played a few bars of music, then stopped the recording and talked about it, Gunno could see what he was trying to teach. It made him think of Ogion, Ged's first and only real teacher in *A Wizard of Earthsea*, the teacher who had tried to give him the strength of character to match his magic powers. Ged had protested that he wasn't learning anything from him. 'Because you haven't found out what I am teaching,' the mage had replied. And because he hadn't understood, the whole disaster of the shadow, and its unleashing, had followed.

At first Gunno hadn't known either what was being taught. It made him think of the credits at the pictures where he just wanted the meaningless words to drift away and leave him with the picture which they seemed only to obscure. He had just wished that the speaker would leave the music to wash over him as he was used to: not study it, not try to understand what was going on in the composer's mind.

But as he listened and got pulled further and further into the teacher's framework he changed his mind. He could see what was being taught: he was being shown that a large part of the first movement was built up on three notes, on three simple notes only. The three notes formed a pattern, but by varying the rhythm and extending the phrase, the composer made of them something quite different. The opening tune had sounded lyrical, but later, with the rhythm quickened, the pattern became dislocated, distorted, the instruments sounding almost angry. He could see at the end of the segment that it was not in variety that the strength of the composition came, but rather in the development of what at first seemed to be quite frugal elements.

He played the tape through again, this time finding it much easier to identify the three notes in all their changes of tone and rhythm. The music, or the effect of it, reminded him in some way of the play of Geoff's that he had watched: the Swedish play about the milk stand. And of course, that was it: in the play too he had been amazed by what amounted to almost a paucity of materials. There was the milk stand and the man's persistence; all else was elaboration.

He had meant to listen to more music or perhaps play a video, but he felt that would spoil the effect of what he had just heard. He lay still, relaxing in the chair, the dog grunting at his feet, and wondered lazily if he should choose a book to read. One of Geoff's this time, maybe. But there was some thought pulling at him: something he had to do.

He hauled himself up and walked out through Geoff's study, out to the verandah and then up the stairs. It was a circular house this – you had to move almost in circles to get anywhere. The little dog followed him, her ball hopefully in her mouth. He ignored the ball but patted the dog when he reached the top of the stairs. She understood and slumped down, her white paws hung over the edge. Then she dropped the ball beside her, its tip leaning precariously over the edge too.

He opened the door and stared into Hugh's room. He didn't feel he could quite face the scrawl of Hugh's writing – not again today. He would look for something else. He moved over to the bookshelves, ignoring the unopened exercise books and text books piled up high on the floor. He was searching – although searching was too strong a word for his desultory looking – not for a book but for something stored as a book: a journal maybe, a nature diary, anything that would give him a clue. Then he spotted what seemed likely: a tall, thick, dark blue book, pushed up against the end of the top shelf. He stood on Hugh's desk chair and lifted it down.

He couldn't believe his luck; he felt his hands tingle as they closed around it. Just as he'd thought: a photograph album. At last he would find out what Hugh looked like at least, for there were no photos of him on the piano or in the bedrooms – the usual places for family photos as Gunno had noticed on raids with the gang.

He looked through the album. But there were no photos that seemed to be of Hugh – only of what must be his mother and father. Most of the photos seemed to be of the dog: the dog as a puppy, lying on the couch, sitting in the sand-pit, chasing a branch of plum blossom, or lying tiny, golden, in a basket. Gunno smiled.

He went carefully through the whole album, turning over the pages, checking that he hadn't turned over two at once, but there was not a single picture of the boy. It could be because Hugh had taken all these photos himself, of course, but then again, there were spaces in the album. Anne must have taken them out, he thought suddenly, or perhaps Hugh himself did. Some people hated photos of themselves: it gave them an eerie feeling. He knew his mother had never liked any of them to be photographed -- once she had even run away from a photographer who had taken a snap of them at the beach. He wondered if she, if Hugh, felt about it as the community of *A Wizard of Earthsea* did about naming: that it weakened you, gave someone power over you. Whatever the reason, the album was empty of photographs of Hugh.

Gunno felt an inordinate disappointment. And maybe he *had* felt that – felt that by having a picture of Hugh, having him defined in that way so that he would no longer have to wonder if he were tall or short, slight or fat, with eyes blue or brown, grey or green like Jess's – having him defined in that way would have given him power not only over the image but over Hugh himself. He always felt uneasy now when he thought of Hugh – as though there were something that needed doing, something even, that *he* had to do.

He went through the album carefully again. It seemed to him that these photographs were mainly, perhaps solely, Hugh's – not just in the sense that they were in his room, but that Hugh had taken them. Quite a few distant shots of the dog, of Anne, even seemed to have been taken from Hugh's own room.

There had been one photo he had flicked past before, but that he now looked at with more interest. It was different from the others and at first had appeared to him to be less significant. Although there were many photographs of the garden in different seasons – but mainly in spring with white and pink blossom hanging thick on the grass, and blue blue skies – they had had something else for a focus. Geoff was really the point of the photograph, or more frequently Anne, or, most frequently of all, the little dog. And once (Gunno looked at this one more closely, indulgently) what must be Hugh's new bike, green like his own but shining, immaculate, glittering with newness. But in every case the garden was a background.

But this photograph was different: it was only of vegetation – the background was the subject. There was nothing in the photograph but trees and undergrowth and glimpses of blue sky. It wasn't part of the garden either: the garden of the big house was a mixture of native and introduced trees and shrubs – peppermint and red gums, ashes and oaks, wattles and roses. But the land in the photo was scrub. What seemed to be the subject was a clump of what looked like stringys on the left of the picture and a patch of high, rather scruffy-looking understorey on the right.

Gunno stared at the picture, puzzled. It seemed a strange thing to make a picture of. He searched it, centimetre by centimetre, looking for some other possible kind of subject: a native animal, a bird, a butterfly, a tiny flower. But there seemed to be nothing.

The picture then was just of trees, just of trees growing out of a high form of scrub. Only of trees, and yet, as Gunno stared at it, he felt a tingle of unease, and shivered a little as if he were cold.

Chapter Nine

The librarian came over to help him. It was a nice day and things were probably a bit slack. 'You seem lost,' she said. 'What were you looking for?'

Gunno flushed. 'Something about trees.'

'Growing them?'

'No. Identifying.'

'Natives?'

Gunno nodded.

'Oh.' Her face brightened. 'I've got just the thing.' She came back with a small moss green paperback. *Know Your Own Trees*, it counselled in white lettering.

'Just the thing,' she said again, beaming, obviously delighted to have matched need with book so perfectly. 'It looks small, but it's amazingly detailed and sensible. I'm sure you'll find what you want in that.'

Gunno rode home past the cemetery, pausing at the entrance, staring again at the sign. But as he sat there on his bike, his feet on the lumpy ground, he got that prickle of unease again, as if someone were watching him. Yet the cemetery was peaceful and still as it always was – as you'd expect it to be. Empty. He looked around at the old gravestones, white, crumbling, tilting out of the earth: two were leaning together like lovers. Then he saw the grass around one of the graves wobble rather than wave. He watched it steadily and smiled to himself.

He propped his bike by the gate and trudged up the slope, sandy and dotted with white marbled stones. Wally was lying on the end grave in the row nearest to the road, and shielded from it by a cluster of peppermints and a spreading olive bush. Gunno crouched down beside him.

'Aren't you going to ask me what I'm doing?' Wally asked, grinning up at him.

'No. I can see what you're doing. You're weeding.'

It was true. Wally was pulling out grass from the little cracks in the crumbly slab and putting them in a neat pile at the side of the grave. It was made of the same white marbled stone as the pebbles on the paths.

'Thought I'd clean up,' said Wally. 'Make it a bit nice. He was only fifteen after all.'

'Fifteen and a half,' corrected Gunno, looking at the headstone. 'Richard James Elsegood,' he said slowly. 'It sounds like a man's name.'

'Pretty crook to die as young as that,' said Wally.

'Some die younger than that. You noticed any boys here younger than that?'

'Nup,' said Wally. 'None. Babies, three-year-olds maybe. No boys. Except Richard.' He patted the stone consolingly.

'"Accidentally killed" it says,' he went on. 'What do you think it would have been? Car accident?'

'It's 1889, Wally,' said Gunno mildly. 'Horse and buggy, maybe. Falling tree. Mine shaft.'

'Snake?'

'No,' said Gunno consideringly. 'No, I don't think it would say "killed" if it were a snake.'

'Why not?'

'I don't know, really.' He tried to think about it although his thoughts kept straying to the small green book that lay waiting in his bag. '"Killed" sounds more sudden, brutal somehow than snake bite. If it were a snake it would say "Died as a result of snake bite". I think it would, anyway. I'm sure I've seen that on some graves out Gawler way. Same with drowning. It would say, "Accidentally drowned".'

'Let's make it a falling tree, then. That would fit in well with summer, wouldn't it? "December 15, 1889".'

'Yes, fits in well,' said Gunno, but absent-mindedly.

'What were you staring at, down at the cemetery gate?' asked Wally.

'You, probably.'

'No. Before that. You were staring up at something.'

'Oh, that. Just the sign – it annoys me.'

'Why?'

'You tell me,' said Gunno. He knew Wally liked puzzles.

Wally came back puffing. 'A cemetery's the one place you'd think you wouldn't need a sign,' he said, searching Gunno's face to see if that were the right answer, 'but if you do, then it's okay, I guess.'

'It's the spelling,' said Gunno. 'It should be cem-e-ter-y.'

'Oh,' said Wally, but without interest. He went back to his weeding.

The day before, at the big house, Gunno had patted the dog quickly, then run straight up to Hugh's room and fetched down the album. He'd had an absurd fear that the photograph would have gone. But it was still there. He'd pulled it out from its plastic sheeting to have a closer look at it – and seen that it had lettering on the back. Well, words, really. Two words. 'Ecal, PYM'. He had stared at them, puzzled, then turned back to the front of the photo and looked again.

But it was just a picture of gum trees – stringys, he

thought. 'Ecal. PYM'. Gunno stared at the letters again, then his face cleared. It was Hugh's wonky old spelling again. The 'Ecal.' would be for 'Eucalypt'. 'Eucal.' he should have written. Funny, he would have expected him to have started the word with a 'u' – the way it sounded. Still, he supposed that someone had carefully taught him that it started with an 'e'. So unexpected would that news have been that he would have dropped the 'u' in despair. 'PYM'. That must be an abbreviation too. Eucalyptus Pygmantha. He was only making it up, but there was bound to be some such name.

He had put the photograph carefully in his pocket, meaning to get a book from the library, meaning maybe, even to show it to Wally. He often thought of Wally as a kind of faded version of Pete. He was blond, but not as blond as Pete; he had blue eyes but not exceptionally blue as Pete's were; he was tanned but not as tanned as Pete; he was good-looking but not as good-looking as Pete. And so the list might go on. The impression was accentuated or perhaps suggested by the fact that Wally often wore Pete's cast-off clothes. Yet at times Gunno suspected that if you could look into their minds, the opposite might be true: Pete might be a kind of faded version of Wally. Wally was sharp.

Thinking about Wally and Pete had reminded him of that strange piece of writing of Hugh's about brothers. He'd read it the other day before he had listened to the Brahms. He pulled the exercise book from its place in the stack in the corner and read it again:

MY BROTHER OR SISTER

My brother or sister doesn't exist. I am what is known as an only child. I wonder if poeple know that when they say that it sounds bad. Self-indulgint, as if its you whose chosen. In some ways maybe it is. I used to wonder if it was becuase I was so aweful as a baby that my parents didn't have any more. After all, most poeple have another one when the first is only a baby and that is all they have to go on. Whatever the reason, I am an only child.

Sometimes I imagine what it would be like to have a brother. Even when I try to imagine him as quite diffrent from myself, he always turns out looking the same or nearly the same, with hair like mine and the same sort of skin. I even imagine him as the same size and looking the same age as me, even though I have made him almost two years yunger.

I imagine him as being queiter than I am and steadier, almost solem, but apreciating when things are funy. One thing that's strange – I keep trying to think of what his name would be, and I can't. I don't think it would have been just a usual sort of a name. I even asked Mum once what she would have called another boy if she'd had one, but she didn't know either. That's how far away she must have been from ever having another one.

So Hugh too recognised the importance of names. He felt uneasy about this imaginary, shifting brother of his partly because he didn't know his name. Gunno thought of *A Wizard of Earthsea*, of Ged pursued by and then pursuing the shadow: the shadow that he, by his arrogant action, had unleashed on the world; not knowing how to deal with it because he did not know its name.

Chapter Ten

The next week was to be one of the most unsettling in Gunno's life, yet it began calmly enough and positively too with a quiet Monday at school and a meeting with Wally in the graveyard.

He'd stopped by the sign on his way home from school. 'You still there, Wally?' he called into the graves.

'Yup,' said Wally. 'But I'm not still here – I've just come back. What do you think I should put in?'

Gunno walked over, bemused, to Richard Elsegood's grave. 'Put in?'

'Yes. Plant. What do you think it would be nice to plant?'

'You mean in the cracks?'

Wally nodded.

'Oh . . . seed?' Gunno imagined Wally shaking the packet in.

'Brilliant. But what kind?'

'Well, you wouldn't want a gum tree. What about a ground cover – a creeper of some sort?'

'That's what I thought. The question is, what sort? It'd have to be hardy. I don't want to have to come back all the time to water it.'

'But you *do* come back all the time,' Gunno pointed out.

There was silence while Wally searched for weeds that might have come up since he'd been there last. 'I wonder what colour I should get,' Wally pursued. 'For my plant, I mean.'

'Of course.'

'Something that would flower for his birthday. I thought since it's a yellow and white cemetery . . .'

'Yellow and white?' said Gunno incredulously.

'Yellow of wattle and white of almond blossom,' said Wally, becoming quite poetic under the force of his enthusiasm. 'I thought it would be nice to get something that has a white or yellow flower.'

'To match the prevailing colour scheme,' said Gunno ironically. He threw in a spanner. 'I don't know, he might be sick of it. He might want a change from yellow. Even from white.'

Wally hadn't thought of that, clearly. Gunno could see his mind skimming over the possibilities, but coming back, with his enthusiasm a little diminished, to his original idea.

'I think yellow,' he said firmly. 'It's a cheerful sort of colour and it fits in.'

'Since you're interested in plants,' said Gunno, seeing his opening, 'what do you make of this?' And he drew the photograph from his pocket. It was curving over slightly: he tried to flatten it with his hands.

Wally stared at it blankly. 'What do you mean? It's just bush, isn't it?'

'Yes, but where? What kind?'

'Could be hundreds of places, couldn't it?' Then seeing, perhaps, Gunno's disappointment, he looked at it more closely. 'It's a bit scruffy. See how high the bushes are. I reckon there's been a fire through – fifteen, maybe twenty years ago. The trees are too skinny yet to keep the bushes down. Is that what you meant?' He stared at Gunno, puzzled.

'Well, I did wonder about the trees. What sort are they?'

'Stringys,' said Wally.

'You don't think they could be Red Box?' He pulled the little moss green book from his other pocket. 'See, it says Red Box most commonly associates with Red Stringybark, but then it says again here,' (he searched again), ' "Bark Compact". You couldn't call stringys compact, could you?'

'Why do you want it to be Red Box?' Wally picked idly at where the weeds had been on the grave.

'Well, the botanical name for Red Box is Eucalyptus Polyanthemos, and here on the back they've written "Eucalyptus PYM". It could be short for that. It could be a . . .' 'Clue,' he had been about to say, foolishly.

Wally lazily took the photo from Gunno's hand and turned it over. 'Doesn't look like "eucalyptus" to me.'

'He's not much of a speller,' said Gunno almost apologetically and without thinking.

'Who isn't?' Wally looked up at him sharply.

'Oh, just some boy.' He went on hastily, 'You see he probably thought "eucalyptus" started with a "u", because of the sound, then someone's told him no, it starts with an "e", so he's got confused and left the "u" off altogether.' Gunno had become quite attached to this explanation by now and thoroughly believed it.

Wally looked casually at the wavery lettering and then, more intently. 'Hey,' he said, grinning broadly. 'I'd say it's much simpler than that. Nothing to do with gum trees.' He stood up and dusted his knees. 'He's spaced the letters like that and put capitals for PYM to put you off the scent. It just says "My Place" backwards.'

Gunno seized the photo and stared at the letters. Wally was right, of course. Why hadn't he seen it for himself? He'd just looked at the letters with that particular set in his mind. My Place. Hugh's place. But Wally was waiting.

'Thanks heaps, Wal,' he said.

'Just call me Sherlock,' said Wally, sticking his stomach out, looking very pleased with himself. 'There was something else too.' He dipped Gunno's arm down so that he could look at the photograph again. 'See that line in the top corner. It could just be a hair on the lens, but it looks too straight for that – I mean, not crinkly. But it's loopy too and thick. I'd say it was a pylon wire.'

So that had been the beginning of Gunno's week, and nothing wrong with that. But then, the next day, he had gone back to the big house.

It was the sort of day, Gunno thought afterwards, that gets your guard down. Even the cars on the main road had seemed to purr rather than roar and a man from the Highways smiled at him as he'd wobbled past the hole they were slowly digging at the side of the road. It was so peaceful, so warm and sunny in the garden with even the birds seeming to be asleep and clouds of insects wavering in front of his face that he was tempted into doing what was really crazy.

'Hi, fella,' he said, patting the dog's long snout as it poked through the cat door. 'You be a good dog and stay quiet now.' And he turned away from the door and went into the garden again. Just for a minute.

The rabbit was stretched out in a corner of his run, mildly opening his eyes as Gunno came up to him. I'd love to lie in that hammock, he thought, looking longingly at it. It was almost concealed from view anyway – hidden by the mulberry tree and screened by the red-leaved prunus. Just five minutes, he thought, with a delicious sense of thrill from doing what he shouldn't. How many days had he come here and no one had come? Who would come? All their friends knew they were both at work.

He pushed his way under the plum trees and rolled himself into the yellow-stringed hammock. Ah, lovely, he thought, gently swinging. Could do with a cushion though. His head lay hard on the strings. Still, he couldn't be going in and out for a cushion, and then he might forget to put it back or he might get a mark on it. He clasped his hands behind his head and rested on them instead.

When he shut his eyes he started to hear the sounds that must have been there all the time. The bees were busy somewhere nearby, maybe in the daisy bushes or in the red gum blossom. There was a constant hum from the road that he hadn't been aware of inside. He was surprised at how loud it sounded. He had imagined this place as being entirely cut off from everything.

The light was soft and dappled here; he looked at the burgundy, at the green leaves. Nothing was ever completely still – the leaves bobbed gently on the spring of their stems, and the light and shadow altered with their movement.

It was warm, far too warm for a jumper. He took it off, a jumper carefully chosen in khaki green – a raid jumper. 'No red,' Jess said, 'no bright blues, no yellow. You want colours that fade into things when you move.' He would never have thought of things like that: Jess was a good leader, a careful leader. It was attention to detail that made you successful. Lazily he rearranged himself in the hammock. He folded his jumper under his head and stretched out with a delicious sense of well-being. This is the life, he thought. And ever so slowly, lightly fingering the photograph still in his pocket, he drifted off to sleep.

It should have been a peaceful dream that he had, there in the hammock, but it wasn't: it was the worst dream he could ever remember. He dreamt that he was in the light – bright light – peering down through a hole into darkness at something, someone. Maybe even at himself. The ground where he knelt was hard, stony, and the hole that he had found seemed to lead down into endless passageways, marked off by high stone walls, that yet led nowhere.

Below him moved the shadow figure feeling his way sightlessly along the walls, his hands black and running with blood. He seemed to be trying to call out. And then even as Gunno watched, helpless, because he did not know the figure's name, he felt the ground slowly begin to tilt and turn over.

It was almost a relief when barking came into the dream although he knew really that thc dog mustn't bark or the figure would never hear him even if he could remember his name. He stood up, suddenly, to quieten the dog and found that he was sitting up in the hammock with it rocking and swaying beneath him. He was sweating all over.

Gunno looked around him, dazed. The labyrinth and the figure had disappeared, but the barking went on. And as Gunno listened to it, still half asleep, he heard another noise: he heard the slam of a car door.

Chapter Eleven

Afterwards Gunno wasn't sure if it hadn't been a dream – the car door slamming and the woman as well. He had looked up, startled, in the direction of the brick path, and seen in bright sunlight a woman, tall with dark hair – a bit like his mother – staring in at him.

He hadn't known what to do – he'd just sat there, at an awkward angle in the hammock, staring back at her in a puzzled way; not knowing whether to run for it, for to run would be to startle her and she was standing so still, almost trance-like. He kept watching her, not sure if he were dreaming. Then she turned and let herself into the house. The dog stopped barking.

That made it seem even more like a dream – that she'd gone away. He picked up his jumper, swung himself out of the hammock and dashed across the lawn, past the sawn-off post and over the little bridge and up to the path above the main road where he had left his bike. The Highways men were still digging the hole: at least one man was digging it while the rest stared into it. And the sun was still high up. He looked at his watch – almost 4.30, 4.27 Wally would say. She'd come home early then. Perhaps she was sick. It was lucky, really, that he'd stayed outside. Just some hammock freak, she might think. Then again it had been so dark in the pittosporums and the patterns of light and shade were confusing. She might think she'd imagined it. Gunno started to wonder if he had – if it had all been part of his dream.

The other thing that went wrong that week was the raid on Ross Road. It went so wrong that Gunno woke the day after it, a Saturday, feeling sick, not wanting to think about it. He would go for a long ride somewhere. Almost like a sleepwalker he wheeled his bike out of his own gate and rode up Rokeby Crescent. But there, by the graveyard, as if he had been waiting for him, sat Wally, the front of his bike turned inwards so that from the distance it looked like a strange animal, grazing.

'Hi, Gunno,' he said, his face lighting up. Then it clouded over. 'Wasn't it awful? How could everything go wrong like that?'

He was talking about Ross Road, of course. Wally wasn't exaggerating: everything *had* gone wrong. Gunno thought back to the second house of the raid. He remembered wiping the perspiration from his forehead, for it was too quiet, this house. The house next door, on the other hand, had been too noisy. There, three Siamese cats had yowled at them so determinedly that they'd got no further in than the kitchen. They'd got nothing there but some loose change scattered about on the green counter.

Wally and Jess were working the top end of Ross Road, Pete and Gunno the bottom. Gunno hated it when he worked with Pete. Pete was jerky, unpredictable. With Wally Gunno could work in a rhythm, steady, calm; but with Pete he felt increasingly uneasy and restless. Take Pete now – he didn't seem to be aware of how silent this house was. He was walking around in it, casually, almost noisily, as if it were his own.

It was a modern house with white painted walls and low ceilings, with blue carpet, blue vinyl. Very clean.

Almost like a hospital, Gunno thought, with the same hushed atmosphere and flowers in a vase in the hall. There were pictures of flowers too, in the lounge and dining-room, and through the bay window he could see the street tree, a splendid jacaranda in full bloom. Dull blue inside, he thought, burning blue outside. This was indeed a blue house.

Pete was bouncing around from room to room opening drawers, clinking jars. Gunno glared at him.

'Keep the noise down, can't you?' he said.

'If you would help,' Pete growled fiercely, 'instead of staring out of windows, it'd be a sight better than telling me what not to do.'

It was true, Gunno thought. Once he had been alert, business-like on a raid. Now he was just as dreamy as if he were at the beach staring at seagulls, or in his house, playing ball up the stairs with the dog.

The passageway went in two directions, with the kitchen, dining-room and lounge coming off the straight stretch that led from the front door. The bedrooms must be on the part that forked to the left. Pete was walking down it now, his footprints showing up on the thick plain pile of the carpet. Gunno followed him slowly, as if caught up in a dream.

He even followed Pete into the first bedroom where Pete had practically finished. Gunno shifted a vase, checked the mattress and under the pillows. Pete was already moving on to the next room, stuffing notes into his jacket pocket and looking better pleased with himself. This first bedroom was just ordinary. It was what they almost always found: a double bed, a wardrobe, a chest of drawers, some photos sitting on it, a mat for a vase. It was the second bedroom that was to be different.

Pete swung confidently into the room, then stopped just as suddenly. Gunno, again following him, saw him freeze. Over Pete's shoulder Gunno tried to see what was wrong. The single bed in the corner was made up and smooth, like a hospital bed. There was a wardrobe, a chest of drawers, another vase of flowers just as you might have expected. It was the chair that was different. There was a high-backed chair in the room, by the window, looking out at the astonishing blue of the tree, and in it sat a white-haired man apparently fast asleep, his knees and feet covered up with a blue plaid rug.

It was what Gunno had always feared. It was the fear that he had had that first time at the big house: that you would come to rob a house only to find that you were sharing it with its owner. Gunno turned and walked silently on the deep piled carpet down the passage, then out to the laundry. He pushed himself through the window, knocking his arm on the frame. He made himself walk down the path past the flaring jacaranda, not even thinking about Pete, then down the steep end part of the street to the main road and sanity and traffic. Only then did he start to run. As he ran all he could think about was the blue plaid rug.

Even now Gunno's stomach turned over when he thought about the raid. And now here was Wally, wanting to talk about it. He let Wally go over and over it, grunting occasionally so that he wouldn't have to talk.

'Pete thinks we should give it a miss for a while. Keep a low . . . something or other.'

'Profile,' completed Gunno.

'That's it. What do you think, Gunno?'

'Give it a miss full stop.'

'You serious?' Wally's eyes opened wide.

'I'm not sure,' said Gunno. 'But I don't want to think about it right now.' He looked steadily at Wally who took the hint.

'You going somewhere, Gunno?'

'Maybe.'
'Can I come?'
'Sorry.' He tried to smile, to soften it.

But soon Gunno had to think about it, about the gang. They were to meet the following Saturday at the beach. He went early, hoping to see Jess.

It wasn't as hard as he thought it would be to tell her. Maybe she could see it in his face. She'd been for a swim and was lying, drying out, on the sand. It was already hot.

He didn't waste time. 'Jess,' he said, 'you asked me what's wrong.'

She raised herself on an elbow, staring into his face.

'I don't think I knew myself then,' he went on. 'What it is, I don't feel the same about the gang. I don't mean about you and Wally and Pete; I mean about what we do. I want to pull out.'

'Is it because of that last raid?' she said, looking a bit white but keeping her voice level. 'You were right. We've been taking risks. Are you scared we'll be found out? That your father will know?'

Gunno paused. Perhaps it would be easier to let her think that – that he was scared, scared of being found out, scared above all of what his father would say. Yes, he supposed he was afraid, afraid of that, although he'd never really thought much about it before. But he'd always known you couldn't get away with that sort of thing for ever.

'It's not that, not just that,' he said slowly, trying to work through the confusion of his motives and find something reasonably convincing and true enough that might satisfy her.

'I'm not happy about it any more.' Curiously it was the image of the little dog he kept seeing, cowering that first time at the head of the stairs. Pete had kicked her into a room.

'Happy?' Now it was Jess's turn to echo.

'Well, it used to seem fun, exciting; and the money was handy.'

'And it isn't any more?'

'Oh yes.' He sighed. 'But I don't like doing it.' He couldn't get closer to it than that.

'You mean it seems wrong?' Her voice was rising so that more than the seagulls were looking at them in an interested way.

He didn't say anything.

'And what does that make us?' she said, her voice shrill with hurt. 'Me and Pete and Wally.'

'Same as before,' he said, trying to calm her. 'Same as before.'

'But you,' she said, 'you're different. You're better.' She said it as if it were the vilest of insults.

'I just . . . don't feel right about it any more. I don't want to do it any more. I want out.' His face settled into mulish lines.

'Fine,' said Jess. 'Great. Who's stopping you? Why don't you just push off?'

'No, I'll wait for Wally and Pete to come. I want to tell them myself.'

'Pete'll flatten you,' said Jess, her voice going hard. 'I wish you'd just go.'

'I'm sorry, Jess.' His voice softened in the old way and she looked away from him down the beach to where the early morning dogs were chasing one another into the sea. He could see that what he had said made her feel diminished, as if he saw them all as petty thieves now – common kids who took what wasn't theirs. All the trappings and rituals that had elevated what they did seemed to be falling away.

'Hi!' Pete and Wally came running across the sand, ending on their bottoms at Jess's feet after a huge skid.

'Sorry we're late,' said Wally. 'We stopped for an icecream.'

He didn't need to explain for his chin was draped with the remnants of a strawberry cone. He rubbed his chin and sand stuck to it. 'Aw, I'm all sticky,' he said. 'I'm off for a dunk.'

The three older gang members watched him go. Pete stretched out lazily in the sand. He was a warm rich golden brown already and his teeth flashed when he spoke. His satiny bathers gleamed against the sand. The other two looked at him glumly.

'What's up?' he said, shaking his hair out of his eyes. It shone bright gold. 'We're not *that* late.'

'Gunno's got something to say,' said Jess.

Pete looked at him. 'You've decided to go to the Antarctic, book in at a private school, leave the gang,' he said, listing what to him were the greatest impossibilities he could think of. He grinned at them, charmingly. Jess didn't smile back.

'Right,' said Gunno, 'on the third attempt.'

Pete went still. 'Don't joke like that about the gang, mate,' he said. 'It isn't funny. Look at the time we've all spent getting this gang right. Nobody pulls out.'

'I just have,' said Gunno.

'Look, I know we bungled that last job,' said Pete, 'but we'll all be more careful now. We got away with it, didn't we?'

'Yeah, we got away with it,' said Gunno flatly.

'Well, what more do you want?'

'I told you,' said Gunno.

'Look,' said Pete again, still trying to be conciliatory. 'Stow it, Gunno. These great plans you draw, the way you remember everything. We couldn't manage without you, you know that.' He appealed to Jess. 'Could we?'

Jess glanced sideways at Gunno's still face. 'Looks like we'll have to. That's how it seems to me.' She pulled herself painfully up and followed Wally out to the surf.

'She's upset, mate,' Pete persisted, lowering his voice and looking earnestly at Gunno. 'We need you in the gang. *She* needs you.'

'I know,' said Gunno. 'That's what makes it so hard.'

'Why you conceited bastard,' said Pete, changing tack at once. 'Don't think we won't manage, for we will. Heaps of kids'd want your job.'

'Yeah,' said Gunno, pulling himself up as slowly as Jess had done. 'I dare say.'

Even Pete could hear the note of blank disinterest in his voice. Gunno was finished with them? All right, they were finished with Gunno. Gunno could see Pete was thinking about laying him out on the sand, but deciding that somehow it didn't seem worth using up all that energy.

'I'll be off, then,' said Gunno. 'Tell Wally I . . .' He looked at Pete's unresponsive face. 'Oh nothing.'

Pete would tell Wally in his own way.

I've made the break, Gunno thought, as he walked up the ramp. I should feel good about it. But of course he didn't. He felt as if his life were slowly emptying around him. Lately he had grudged the time and the effort that the gang activities had involved, for they had taken his thoughts away from the house. Yet how much longer could he go there? He had already been seen. But as he walked away from the beach, away from the gang, away from Jess, he realised why he was feeling so awful. He felt like a traitor.

Chapter Twelve

The next day was cold, unseasonably cold, with a threat of rain, but Gunno knew he had to do something. He couldn't sit at home brooding about the gang. He took Hugh's photo out of the book where he had been flattening it, put it carefully in his parka pocket, then zipped it up.

He wobbled past the cemetery, carefully not looking in at the blank grave where Wally wouldn't be, and pushed his way against the wind to the turn-off into Hawthorndene. He passed the oval and the tennis courts, then got off his bike where the road turned abruptly at a right angle and shot practically straight up into the air. This part was far too steep for his bike. He glanced at his watch, then walked up and up past the houses to where the golf course began. He got on his bike again, the wind coming at him in gusts, and followed the twist of the road, pasture and gums, till it opened up in scrub at the top of the hill.

The bush was tangled-looking and mainly stringy bark, as he'd remembered it, yet he had a dismal sense of wrongness as he stared around him. Where could he even begin to search? He had already discounted the land to the left of him. It was part of the National Park. *Some place on your own.* Hugh would hardly have decided to have his own place in a public park, however big it was. Then on the right . . . The sky was overcast and the scrub looked grey, uninviting, with barbed wire all the way along it as far as he could see. This place was too far away and somehow not private enough. It had the wrong feel.

He kept thinking of Jess, white-faced and angry. Jess was never angry – never *had* been angry, he corrected his thoughts. He searched for a word that would describe her – not when she was angry, but as she normally was. Statuesque, that was it. Jess was far better than pretty. And her eyes were extraordinary – green as the sea was sometimes. Her hair, he supposed, wasn't extraordinary. It was a comfortable, unspectacular blond but thick and long. A shade lighter and it would have been yellow, a shade darker, a fairish brown. Pete's hair was golden and Wally's whiter – like a bleached, a faded version of Pete's – but he liked Jess's colour more. It seemed dependable.

He forced himself not to think of her. Once he had liked the thought of her. She had made him want to laugh – not that he would ever have shown her that. She was so determined and methodical, such a perfectionist. It was funny being a perfectionist at what they did, but she was. That was why they had been so successful, so successful until now.

He rode back with the wind, fast and bending almost recklessly into the curves. He caught glimpses of the sea. He tried to think of Hugh again, of the scrub. The scrub here had been right but not the place. Somewhere easier. It couldn't be the Clarendon road; that was all pasture now with just small patches of scrub left – little more than verge. Somewhere else, then, near at hand. He raced down the last steep slope. His face burned in the wind.

He couldn't believe it at first, that it could be him. But as he cycled nearer he could see that it was: Wally, leaning against a post at the Hawthorndene oval, his face small and tight-looking in the cold. 'Hi,' he said, unsmiling. 'I saw you go past and called out, but you didn't hear, maybe, in the wind.'

'No,' said Gunno gently, 'I didn't hear.'

'That's the wrong way. It's too steep for too long. I thought of a place. You're looking for that place in the photo, aren't you?'

Gunno nodded. Why pretend?

Wally raised his eyes to Gunno's for the first time. 'Then try Rutland Hill. See you.'

Gunno watched him go. The kid'd waited for him – waited for him to come back. Stood in the cold in a T-shirt, all that time. Rutland Hill. He would try it, like Wally suggested. But not today.

He wheeled his bike over the bits of white rock and the bright green mosses at the side of the road to the broken down part of the fence. To his left the pylon rose rigid to the sky, the light dancing on the wires that plunged down one slope and up the next to a further pylon. He walked in, past a line of stringys, to an almost flat area of pasture grass dotted with black boys and black-trunked wattles.

It was only when the ground started to slope steeply downwards that the bush properly began. The understorey was high – three to four metres in parts – and out of it rose grey clumps of stringys. He dropped his bike as soon as the slope hid him from the road and walked in. The ground was thick with branches and leaves, and crackled loudly every time he took a step. It wasn't easy to push through the black boys and the spiky hakea bushes. He had to keep finding simpler ways around the tangle of the bush.

At the bottom of the first slope, before the land fell away again, there was an area of flat, with a creek bed and some blackberries following its course. He stood looking up at the trees around him. Some were enormously tall, like the two red stringys next to him. The third of the group had fallen, and he sat down on it. He looked up at the two remaining, so tall and yet with such a tiny top knot of foliage. It made him think of giraffes. To the right was a grove of native cherries, and near there, but further into the flat area, someone had dug out a waterhole, its edges straight and red.

He walked over to it and stared in. It was dark and muddy but drew your eyes the way water always did. Idly he broke up a stick and plopped it in the water, watching the ripples form and the images dissolve and return. The place was full of birds. Now as he listened he could pick out the clear note of the rosella, the cry of the black cockatoo. He could even see blue wrens, over by the native cherries, flitting and diving in the way he knew they did.

He looked around him with growing disappointment. It would be easy here, to compose a photograph with the wire, the stringys, the high understorey. It was the right kind of land with the right kind of feel. He had felt quite sure – oddly certain – as he had pushed through the broken bit of the fence that this was the right spot: Rutland Hill as Wally had suggested. And then he had found it, he had felt so sure, by the pylon just before Woodsman's Drive.

But he had expected some sort of revelation, something – he wasn't quite sure what. A cubby-house maybe, amateurishly constructed out of fallen branches, a tent, a pile of books – *something* left behind. But there was nothing visible like that: no sign at all. Only, now that the birds had fallen silent a strange waiting feeling seemed to have fallen on the bush. He shivered although it was now so hot.

Chapter Thirteen

Gunno stayed away from the big house as long as he could, which was ten days. Then he found himself having to go back. He'd watched it though, for several days. It was possible that Anne had lost her job, or was on holiday. He had to be sure that that early home-coming wasn't likely to happen again. As he watched, afternoon after afternoon, he'd wished he'd had a dog. If you had a dog you could take it with you and it would sniff everywhere and no one would look at you twice. It was more difficult, looking casual, without one. He would like to have a dog – yet he knew that the only one he wished for was the dog inside the big house.

He walked past the well that sat so neatly inside the red brick path, and found his eyes attracted upward to a blaze of gold. The silky oak was flowering, its huge horizontal blossoms swaying in the light wind.

He let himself into the house, cautiously, fearfully, as if it were for the first time. The little dog was there to welcome him, jumping up on him, putting her paws over his hands so that he wouldn't move away, her face adoring, eager. She pranced away to bring him her red ball.

He wandered through the house touching things, reminding himself of them, trying to recapture the peace that the house had always brought him. The little dog kept following him, jumping up whenever he paused.

He walked into Hugh's room, feeling that slight catch of his breath as he opened the door. But the room lay empty before him as it always did, with its bright carpet, red quilt cover and its blinds, red too, but sobered with a clear blue. He went to the bookshelf and searched for something to read. He pulled out *The Tombs of Atuan* from where it still sat packaged with *The Farthest Shore* and curled up with it on Hugh's bed.

At first he'd liked it, but in a dreary sort of way for the landscape had changed, had diminished so much since the Earthsea book. Earthsea had encompassed islands and seas, but this story was set in desolation, amid crumbling rock and earth, and was filled with images of waste and darkness and dust.

But as he read on his mild interest changed to something akin to horror. As he turned page after page – feverishly, sometimes reading ahead, knowing increasingly what he would find – he felt himself break out into a sweat. The story disturbed him, *frightened* him more than anything he had ever read. He closed the book suddenly and put it back on the shelf. But the feeling of it seemed to hang in the air: the musty air of Hugh's bedroom seemed full of the smell of earth.

He walked slowly to Anne's study, trying to think sensibly about it. He would have to write to his mother about the book, especially about that dream he'd had. He'd take some of Anne's paper – just borrow it – and use her pen.

Usually when he wrote to his mother he put the address and the date in a spread out sort of way at the top, to take up space. But today he had something to say. But how was he going to say it? He stared out of the window at the silky oak. The swaying blossoms looked disconnected from one another, some smaller, some in what appeared to be broken lines, but all moving in the same direction like great ripples on a lake or waves at sea.

He stared next at the plum tree, its branches crowding in to the window. Someone had lopped a branch of it – maybe a year ago, maybe two. Gunno imagined how stark it must have looked at the time: now there were little branches going out from it all up the amputated branch. Most of them were growing on one side – towards the window. Gunno wondered why that should be. He would have expected it to be the opposite, with them all reaching out for the sun. But nothing grew from the end of the branch. The little branches waved gently at him, then more determinedly as the wind took them.

He sighed and looked at his letter. Then he threw himself into Anne's armchair, away from the window, and looked at it again. He didn't want to tell her – not really, for it would be to admit at last what he had always suspected, had always avoided. He was like her: at least in one respect he was like her. In any case there was no one else he could tell. And there seemed to be a growing urgency about it, a growing sense that there was something he had to do – that only he *could* do – and that if he didn't do it soon, it would be too late.

'Dear Mum,' he wrote, in sprawling capitals . . .

The little dog sat up suddenly and started to growl. Then she scrambled to her feet, barking and barking. And now Gunno could hear it too. There was someone at the door. He got up, his letter falling to the floor, and crawled into the bedroom where he couldn't possibly be seen from a window while the dog ran down the stairs, frantic. But the knocking went on.

Then suddenly – even more frighteningly, it stopped. It stopped and a strange hush fell. Gunno strained his ears for footsteps heading across the red bricks, crunching up the drive. But there was no sound that way at all. Whoever it was must have gone round the other side – to cross the lawn or to hammer at the dining-room door. But there was no sound of further knocking. He listened, uneasy, his head down to catch the least sounds. The dog had come upstairs again, and was defending the house from her usual position at the top. She was growling continuously, low in her throat, her ears well back. He moved out beside her.

And from there he could hear something: a subdued sort of rustle coming, he thought, from the dining-room. It was only then, with rising panic, that he remembered: he'd opened the door briefly to air the room, then it had blown shut and he'd forgotten to lock it. Someone had come in through the dining-room door.

He tiptoed into Anne's bedroom and took a couple of books from the pile at the side of the bed; it would be something to use, something to hurl at the intruder. Then back, his heart thudding, to the top of the stairs. The dog had started barking again but he could still hear the sound of light footfalls. He watched, terrified, as the kitchen door opened slowly wider, but it was someone smaller than he had been expecting who stood there.

'What you waiting for, Wal?'

Gunno could hear Pete's voice from the kitchen, but Wally just kept staring up at him, completely silent. The dog pounded down the stairs, snapping at Wally's legs. Pete aimed a kick at her and tried to push past Wally to see what he was gaping at.

'Leave the dog alone!' yelled Gunno, hurtling down the stairs, almost to the bottom, just as Jess came bolting round the kitchen door and into the pack of them.

'Get out!' yelled Gunno. 'Get out of here! How dare you come back here!'

'Listen to him,' sneered Pete. '"How dare we!" Who does he think he is, the hypocrite. I thought you said no more stealing from houses . . .'

'That's what I said.'

'Then why're you here?' said Wally, his voice almost a squeak. 'You wanted all the loot for yourself, didn't you?'

Gunno looked over his head at Jess. She was staring at him, shocked. 'Is that it, Gunno?'

'You know it's not,' he said tersely, sweeping his hand across his face as if that would wipe them all away.

'What you doing, then,' said Pete, 'sneaking into houses?'

'I'm not sneaking into houses,' said Gunno. 'I'm not sneaking anywhere. Now get out, all of you, before I call the police.'

'Hark at him!' said Pete. 'Call the police! And what about you? What are you doing here? Guarding the house with that silly yellow pooch.'

The dog had shrunk away a little now, but was still barking sporadically from a corner of the verandah.

'Yes, I suppose so,' said Gunno, drawing himself up. 'I suppose I am. And it's a brave dog – not yellow at all. Now get out, all of you.'

Jess was staring fixedly at him. She would be thinking that he should look guilty, caught out. But he knew he didn't. He didn't even look embarrassed. Wally's face was puckering up as if he might cry. Suddenly he reached behind him and grabbed a pot plant and hurled it at Gunno's head. The earth broke all over him. He shook the dirt out of his eyes and straightened just in time to see Pete swinging a punch at him. He ducked.

'No, Pete,' said Jess, trying not to yell. 'Don't start fighting now. Talk about asking for trouble.'

And without looking at Gunno, she pulled Pete after her through the kitchen door. She only turned for long enough to see that Wally was following.

The door thudded behind them. Gunno locked it, then bent down to comfort the dog. She was following him everywhere.

'You did a good job, Sam. What a clever dog you were!' He tried to put cheer and conviction into his voice for he loved the dog and she had done her best against those thugs. He examined the word he had used to himself – 'thugs'. Too strong maybe, for Jess anyway, looking so fresh and business-like in her green dungarees and green check shirt. Fancy them coming back here, *knowing* about the dog. Just because it had been a good haul that last time. He felt quite angry with them – some sort of gang it was turning into now.

He walked through the kitchen to the stairs. He looked at the mess of earth, at the plant lying on its side. It was the one that he had faithfully watered. Nothing had ever got damaged in the house before: he had only improved things. He looked at the broken stem of the plant and had an absurd desire to cry.

Chapter Fourteen

He'd felt ill after they'd gone: not able to do anything, not even to go away. He'd lain down on Hugh's bed, his eyes searching out the clear blue of the blinds as if his eyes were sore. He would just lie still for a while. His head felt heavy, almost as if he were going to have a headache quite soon, and his eyelids kept shutting against what seemed to be the glare of the room.

But incredibly, he'd fallen asleep; fallen asleep and had the dream again: that frightening dream he'd had first in the hammock. The same as before, with the hole and the trapped shadow figure, though now it was worse. For this time, after the ground had seemed to tilt, earth then pebbles then rocks had fallen in on the figure in the maze and it seemed, puzzlingly, on himself as well.

It was much later when he woke, but not too late. The brightness of the room had gone but he still had time if he went now. He forced himself to sit up and shook his head. Hugh's red quilt lay tumbled on the floor. He felt awful, sweating, with a sick taste in his mouth and a pounding headache. The dog was asleep on the rug beside him but started to beat her tail into it when he spoke to her.

'Time I was heading off, Sam,' he said. Yet he still sat there, looking drearily at the shelf of books, searching out *The Tombs of Atuan*.

He patted the dog and looked at his watch. Six o'clock. He really must go. He had never stayed as late as this. He brought the dog out of the room with him and shut the door, walked down the stairs and locked the back door behind him.

He looked up at the silky oak, its blossoms almost gold-pink in the changing light. He sat down on the well for a moment, just to look at it. The lid on the well was made of wooden planks, warm and comforting. He glanced at his watch – almost 6.15. 6.13, Wally would have said. But he didn't go even then. He sat on as if hypnotised, gazing at the bright gold of the tree. He was still staring at it when he heard the crunch of tyres on the gravel at the front gate.

Even that hardly startled him. He got up, looked calmly down the red brick path and, seeing no one, walked quite slowly out of sight, round the side of the house and across the lawn.

He remembered thinking, for he was still half asleep, that it would be all right: when Anne and Geoffrey got to the path they would find the well quite empty of boys but the silky oak would still be there. He looked at his watch: it was 6.29 precisely.

It was the following morning. Gunno had never known such blank depression. Usually if he felt bad one day, in the morning it would have lifted. But today he felt worse than he had last night. Maybe no one had seen him leaving the well. But it was finished anyway. The gang had finished it for him. He thought painfully of the house, of the little dog. Maybe if I get on my bike, he thought; ride around. It was still early, cool and fresh, although it was going to be a hot day.

But as he went round the side to get his bike he saw Wally waiting for him at the front fence, standing absurdly with his fists up. Gunno walked up to him without speaking. His face was level with Gunno's chest.

'Come across to the park,' said Gunno at last. 'Let's have a talk.'

Wally hit him then, the punches landing around his waist.

'If you want to fight, it's even more important we go to the park,' said Gunno, side-stepping past him and walking quickly across the narrow road. Wally followed, throwing punches at his back as he took the small track down past the green timber see-saw and swings. There was no one around.

Gunno walked on past the oak tree and over the creek to the stone table and stone seat. It was a memorial to the first school master of the district. Gunno sat down and pretended to read the lettering, waiting for Wally to calm down. But he didn't. He had briefly stopped but now he started punching Gunno again. He hit him round the shoulders, then started on his head. 'Get up,' he said, half crying. 'Get up and fight.'

Gunno stood up and rubbed his neck. 'It's not like you thought,' he said, looking at him sadly and not even trying to get out of the way of the helpless punches. 'Then again I don't think I could explain.'

'It doesn't need much explaining,' said Wally, his voice shrill. 'You were going raiding on your own – to get it all, weren't you? And you didn't have to. I only do it if I have to. Always.'

Gunno had only been half listening, deliberately, to let the words of accusation just slide away. But he'd heard the last words all right. 'What do you mean, you only do it if you have to?'

'Go it alone. Like you were. I don't do it unless I have to.'

'How could you do that to Jess?' Gunno looked at him, his grey eyes cold as the sea in winter.

'I knew you'd look like that,' said Wally. 'I used to feel awful. I used to think, what if Gunno finds out? He'll look at me that way. And you're just as worse as me.'

'Just as bad,' Gunno corrected him absent-mindedly.

'There, you've admitted it,' said Wally triumphantly.

'No. I meant the word, the word you used was wrong.'

'You're all words,' said Wally bitterly.

'When you . . . go it alone, do you wear a kind of boy scout outfit?' Gunno remembered seeing Wally in something puzzling one day, shorts and a shirt in a hideous khaki green with a sort of brownish cap over his soft blond hair. It had been such a hot day too – Gunno had wondered why he was wearing a cap.

'I don't need to tell you anything,' said Wally. 'You're just a . . .' He searched for the word that his brother had used.

'Hypocrite,' said Gunno. 'But Pete's wrong. I've never "gone it alone". What a rotten thing to do.'

Wally turned scarlet. 'Don't you tell me what's rotten. I used to think . . . but Pete's worth ten of you, twenty. And Jess liked you – she was *gone* on you. She liked you better than Pete even.' He said it as if it were some kind of miracle.

'Look, Wally,' said Gunno. 'Don't say any more. We're only making it worse, can't you see? Maybe later, when you're not so angry . . .' His head was starting to pound, and the plum trees around them in the reserve were taking on a double outline.

'I don't want to talk,' said Wally. 'I want to fight. Why won't you fight me?'

'Because . . .' Gunno paused and looked at him quite kindly. He knew that Wally was waiting for him to say something that would really enrage him: because you're smaller than me, because you're younger, because you're not worth fighting with, or even worse, perhaps, because fighting never solves anything.

'Because,' said Gunno at last, 'you are my friend.'

He saw that Wally could have killed him for that. He wouldn't even let him hate him with a pure hate. He watched as Wally walked away, kicking at the oak tree, banging the see-saw and thrusting at the swings so that they swung for a long time after in wild discordant arcs.

Gunno stayed in the park long after Wally had gone, sitting on the stone seat motionless, as if he too were part of the memorial to the Reverend Samuel Gill. After a time he rubbed his arms and flexed his back. Wally's muscles were certainly building up. Maybe he wouldn't be just a faded version of Pete that way either.

He remembered back to the day at the beach. Pete had been picking on Wally in the elder brother way he had. He'd gone on and on about that skate board. 'How come you got enough to buy one?'

Wally had flushed. 'Guess I'm just careful with *my* money,' he'd said, after a pause, meaning that Pete wasn't.

'Yeah, Scrooge,' Pete said.

But when Pete had brought it up again later he remembered trying to help. 'It's good how money adds up,' Gunno had said. 'Two dollars here, fifty cents there, keep it like Wally does, it builds up into a pile.' He'd moved the sand into a mound as if to illustrate his point. 'What kind d'you want to get?'

That had shifted everyone's attention to something else and he could see that Wally was grateful. And all the time ...! He'd thought it was just Pete in his bullying role, and he'd been wrong, or partly wrong anyway. Pete had been right. And Jess? 'Gone' on him. He explored the word. Funny thing for Wally to say, yet Wally would say anything today, and some of it wrong. She liked him, that was closer to it. *Did* like him, he corrected himself. She wouldn't be thinking much of him now.

He felt he was at the end of a lot of things. It was the end of the HBS – Home Burglary Service – 'Homes neatly and professionally burgled. Satisfaction or a money back guarantee'. It was Wally's name and Wally's joke.

It was the end of the house and the end of the little dog. Still, it had never been his house, never been his dog, and he'd been wanting out of the gang. But he'd wanted out of the gang because of the house, and now there was no house to get out of the gang for. Yet he didn't want to go back to that: he felt differently about it all now. Because of the house he had become somebody else. Just because you looked the same, people thought you were the same. But it wasn't true. He would miss Jess. And how he would miss the house. And he was still plagued by the thought that there was something that had to be done: something that *he* had to do. Something to do with the house.

So his thoughts circled and circled in a seemingly smaller and smaller space until he could feel his head starting to split. At least that would give him something to do. He'd go inside, he thought, slowly, wearily, like an old man, and get a Disprin or whatever else his father had bought last and hidden in the cupboard. Then he'd put it in a glass of water, and his father would say, emerging bleary-eyed from the bedroom,

'Painkillers? A young boy like you! What are you doing with a headache at this hour in the morning? Fine start to my day off.'

He walked through the park, past the swings that were hanging still now, up the path and into his house. In the kitchen he dropped the tablet into the water, watched it fizz and bubble, then drank it down, wrinkling his nose at the sick taste of it. His father came through from the bedroom slowly, looking as awful as Gunno felt. He saw the glass on the sink with the traces of powder in the bottom, the foil from the tablet lying crumpled beside it. He sniffed the glass suspiciously. 'Painkillers? At this hour in the morning. A young boy like you.' People were so predictable.

That was the word he'd used to the gang. 'It's our strength,' he'd said, 'that people are so predictable.' He wondered about it now, as he thought about Wally.

Chapter Fifteen

Gunno sat at the top of the stairs with the dog. Her white feet hung over the edge of the step. He stroked them, first one and then the other. She licked his hand, and then, when he had finished, she licked the white parts of her feet. 'What a dog you are for keeping clean feet,' he said to her. 'More like a cat than a dog. You'll still keep it up, won't you fella, when I'm not . . .'

He had come for the last time. He wouldn't come again. He looked down the stairs. The ancient yellow curtain stretched meagrely over the back verandah windows, misted over. He blinked. Never, he thought. I'll never come here again. He counted the stairs. One, two, three, four – there were sixteen stairs. Usually Anne just seemed to clean half of them – maybe it was because that was as far as the cord of the vacuum cleaner stretched and she was too lazy to plug it in again from the top.

I wish . . . he thought. But what did he wish? Wish that he'd never come here? He hadn't wanted to, strongly he hadn't wanted to, but then he hadn't stopped them either. 'There's a dog,' he'd said, but then he'd added, 'but it doesn't bark.' The door had even been open – it had almost been too easy. But now of course he could see it hadn't really been easy at all. If you fell in love with something, a house, a dog, then you had to take the consequences. One day you would lose it, whatever it was. He tried to think of all the happiness he had had in the house – the times of peace, of pure happiness, even playing with the dog and her soft, spiky red ball. Finding out about Anne, almost as if he were her cleaning lady; at least finding out the same sort of things that a cleaning lady would. Finding out about Hugh, and the secret of that musty room, though he still didn't really know. Only that Hugh hadn't come back. Only that there was something he still had to do.

Yet now that the happiness was to end it seemed he wished that it had never happened at all. It was all far too much to lose. Yet, the thought niggled at him, it had never been his properly to have. He had been an intruder here. But it had never seemed like that, at least not after that first time, in a way not even then. The house had seemed to welcome him as if there were a gap there, as if he truly belonged. It was *his* house, it was *his* dog. He looked at the little dog. She was gazing at him with complete devotion, her dark brown almond eyes heavy and liquid with love.

He thought of the little dog waiting in the empty house, waiting for him to come back. If only he could tell her, if only he could explain. Now there would be no one coming home, not till Anne and Geoff came back at 6.28. He still remembered Wally's time. Wally was so precise – not 6.30 as anyone else would have said, but 6.28. It seemed a small thing, two minutes, but it was the sort of precision that had made the gang work for so long so well. He felt differently about it now but still with a kind of admiration for something difficult that had worked perfectly. 'We are professionals,' Jess was always saying. 'We do a professional job.' He thought, oddly, of *Swallows and Amazons* (Christmas,

1984). If he and Jess and Wally and Pete had had a boat, it wouldn't have happened at all.

The little dog would be alone until precisely 6.28 every night. In winter it was dark at five. She would wait all day as the light shifted and the shadows fell and then even darkness and he would not come. And he could not explain to her now why this would happen or that it was not what he had wanted. He buried his face in the thick hair of her back and wept.

He rubbed the backs of his hands into his eyes like a much younger child and sat up. He thought he had heard something. He had had a queer feeling since he had come that there was something wrong with the house. Now he decided it was because it had a listening quality, as if someone were in it. Someone apart from himself.

Yet he had been in most places in the house today – except Hugh's room. He was leaving that till last. The door was shut as usual. He stared at the door, then patted the dog on the head and got up, very slowly. Always when he put his hand on the handle he was aware of a tightening around his heart, but today it felt worse. He waited, hardly able to breathe. Suddenly, annoyed at himself, he pushed the door open, then stood back, looking cautiously into the widening space of the room.

The door swung open as usual on the blinds, on the desk, on the bed . . . Gunno stared in disbelief. There *was* someone – someone lying on the bed, someone with dark hair. He stood quite still in the doorway, feeling his knees collapsing under him, the blood draining away from his face.

But it was a woman. And now she sat up, infinitely slowly, like a corpse might do from a coffin. Gunno felt a scream building up inside him. But it can only be

Anne, he told himself. He thought of her coffee cups and the dead flies. It can only be Anne. This dark pale woman is Anne. And the dog was standing beside him and didn't bark.

She was staring at him, on and on. 'You're a real boy, then,' she said at last. 'And you've been crying. You do exist.' She got up and moved closer to the door.

He looked at her, not saying anything.

'You're not a bit like Hugh,' she said, sounding disappointed, as if it were an accusation. She squinted a bit, trying to look at him more closely. 'Your colouring's the same, your height and build's the same but your face . . . It was you, all the time?'

He looked at her, silent.

'Do you talk?' She was starting to sound angry now, upset and angry at the same time.

I could run away, he thought, but how could I do that? He looked at the large puffy circles under her eyes that seemed to have been stuck there to make her look older.

'Yes,' he said.

'Then talk to me. Tell me what you've been doing in my house. Oh, I know *what* you've been doing. You've been tidying up, watering the cyclamen – by the way what happened to it? – brushing the dog. Do you think I haven't noticed?'

He stared at her.

'Do you realise,' she said, and now she sounded furious, 'do you realise that I thought I was going mad?'

He started at this. Crazy, mad, not normal, peculiar, were words that he shrank from, always.

'"Hallucinating" my husband called it. He said that because Hugh hadn't come back I was hallucinating, imagining that he had. I've seen you three times – in my study, on the well, in the hammock. It was you, wasn't it?'

He nodded.

She looked distressed now, rather than angry. 'Are you *sure* it was you in the hammock? I could have sworn . . . Was that you too?'

He was starting to tremble. 'It was me,' he tried to explain, 'but it was dark in there.'

'Then why didn't you act afraid? Why didn't you run?'

'I don't know . . . I'd been asleep. It seemed part of a dream.'

'And on the well? You didn't run then either.'

'No.' He couldn't explain how he'd felt.

'All right then,' she said. 'I'm not really asking *what* you have done here, I'm asking why? Why have you done it? Why have you come here?'

'I don't know,' he started to say, but he could see from her face that that wasn't fair. She was angry again, angry at him for coming, perhaps angry at him for not, after all, being Hugh. 'It's hard to put into words.'

But she must have seen that he meant to try for she said in a softer voice, 'It's ridiculous, standing here. Come out and sit on the well and tell me, there.'

The dog, quiet and puzzled-looking, followed them outside.

He looked up at the silky oak, waning now, the bright gold gone. 'It was the house,' he said.

'The *house*?'

'I wanted to be in the house.'

'Why?'

'I liked it.' He tried to go painfully on. 'I wanted to be in it alone, and then I wanted to look after it. And the dog, he was part of it. He's a nice dog.'

'She. It's a she,' she corrected him. She looked at the dog who was lying now with her head in Gunno's lap.

'So you liked the house,' she said slowly, wonderingly, trying to make sense of it. 'And you wanted to be in it alone.'

He nodded, looking down at the bricks.

'Do you want to be alone in *all* the houses that you like?'

She must be thinking he was a sort of house buff, house freak.

'This is the only house I like,' he said.

'Why?'

He turned and looked up at the house. His shoulder brushed against the grape vines. The house rose tall towards the sky, towards the huge river red gums across the street. The light was changing already, becoming richer. It made the stone look mellow, glowing.

Gunno didn't say anything: he just looked at the house, then at Anne, then at the house again. She looked sad. 'Yes,' she said, 'I see what you mean. Hugh loved it too.'

'Your son,' Gunno stated. He wondered if he could ask her about that photo, about that land.

'My son,' she said. 'Why did you water the white cyclamen and not the others?'

He smiled, for the first time. It was a slow smile and rather did for his face what the evening sun had done for the face of the house. 'It seemed to deserve it more,' he said. 'I would have done the others but . . .'

'But what?'

'Well, it sounds . . . crazy, but I thought *one* you won't notice, more you will.'

'It was true to think that,' she said. 'I did notice but I thought it was tougher, and then I thought that Geoff . . .'

She had been gazing out past the snowball tree at the little stone house where it nestled into the slope at the edge of the pittosporum grove. Once someone in the house had kept butter there, before there were ice boxes and fridges. Gunno knew that from his history class.

He had noticed it and not noticed it before. But now she turned and really looked at him.

'Why did you write that letter?' she asked him, sounding angry again.

'What letter?'

'It was lying on the floor of my study – the little green room I mean, at the top of the other stairs. "Dear Mum," it began.'

'And finished,' said Gunno wryly. 'I was trying to write to my mother.'

He thought how careless of him, to leave it there. Still, what did it matter now?

'You have a mother?' She said it as if he were a changeling. 'Then why did you put our address at the top? And it was printed too, like Hugh . . .'

He put his head in his hands. 'I'm sorry,' he said. 'It was a mistake. I didn't know I had.'

He thought, how awful! She had thought she was getting a letter from . . . Blast his carelessness. It *had* mattered: it had all mattered far more than he had realised. What had he done here?

She was looking at him, sadly this time. 'I'm afraid it'll have to stop – this babysitting the house,' she added, in case he hadn't understood. 'I can see that you haven't done any damage. You've even helped. I can see that the dog likes you.'

Gunno knew that was an understatement. The dog was lying on the bricks now but she was trying to lick his sneakers from where they dangled down the side of the well.

She was still speaking. 'But it won't do. You must see that.'

'Of course,' said Gunno. He'd known it was over. Once he was found out, it was over. And he had already been found out by the gang.

'But I'd like you to stay till my husband comes home. I need him to see you. I'll explain, it'll be all right. Do you need to make a phone call or anything?'

Gunno shook his head. The phone would only echo in an empty house. His father wouldn't be home for hours yet. When he did come, there'd be the noise of the door opening and the smell of take-away together.

'Then come in the kitchen and I'll make a cup of tea. Tea for you or something else?' She looked vaguely in the fridge. 'I've got out of the way of buying cordial or soft drink.'

'Tea'll be fine,' he said, following her in and sitting uneasily on the green kitchen stool where he had perched comfortably, at home, only an hour or so before. He looked around him at the cream-patterned vinyl, the white counter tops and the dark ceramic tiles above them; at the huge old stove and the little windows cut out on either side of it that let in views of the loquat tree and the lawn behind it. He could tell already how bad he was going to feel. Everything was taking on an air of unreality – the woman, the kitchen, even the dog.

'I think,' he said slowly, levering himself off the stool, 'I think I'll have to go.'

She looked concerned, stared anxiously at her watch. 'He'll be here in a minute. It's not a trick. He won't . . . I mean, I just want him to see you, that's all. I'll explain it to him after you've gone.'

He sat down heavily.

'Milk in it?' she asked. 'Sugar?'

'Just milk. A little. No sugar. Thanks.' He wondered how he could care about that now – that he only took a drop of milk in tea.

She passed him a mug in earth colours with a black jagged design along its rim. 'Really,' she said, 'he won't be long.'

The tea was too hot yet to drink. He held onto the mug with both hands, his knuckles white, forcing himself to keep still. There was something he'd been meaning to ask, something important – about Hugh. But his mind had gone hopelessly blank. He looked down at the dog, feeling trapped, feeling desperate, waiting for her ears to go back, waiting for the first sign that Geoffrey had come home.

Chapter Sixteen

Gunno didn't look up. He stood in the kitchen, staring at the floor. The dog had stopped barking and was jumping up on the man's legs: on Geoffrey's legs, the man who watched films about milk stands.

'There *is* a boy,' Anne had said without any preliminaries when her husband had come inside. She put a hand on Gunno's shoulder. 'Hugh and not Hugh, as you see.'

Gunno stood still, his head down, like an exhibit.

There was silence. The dog slunk past, looking uneasily at Gunno, then curled up in her basket in the corner of the kitchen. It would have her blue blanket and her red spiky ball in it. Geoffrey put his briefcase down on the counter and turned to Gunno.

'What have you been doing in my house?' His voice was harsh.

'It's all right, Geoff,' said Anne. 'He's told me about it. He just liked it here. He liked the house. I'll tell you later – I just wanted you to see him.'

'You *liked* my house.' He ignored Anne and kept talking to Gunno. 'And how did you get to like it, eh? What were you doing here in the first place? *Look at me, boy*.' He paused. 'Do you like *money* too?'

Gunno looked up very slowly. Geoffrey was shorter than he'd imagined, stocky, with grey sprinkled everywhere through his black hair. He was shorter than Anne. She was gripping Gunno's shoulder more firmly. 'Don't talk to him like that,' she said. 'He hasn't taken anything.'

'Hasn't he?' Geoffrey's tone was contemptuous. 'What about that break-in?'

'It wasn't you, was it?' said Anne kindly. 'Of course it wasn't.'

Gunno dug his nails into his palms. She would be thinking it couldn't be anyone who looked so like her son. It would be so easy to deny it.

'Well?'

Gunno stared at the floor again. 'Yes,' he said.

Anne's arm faltered on his shoulders.

'Yes what?' said Geoffrey.

'Yes, it was me but . . .'

'You'll never do it again?' Geoffrey's tone was cynical. 'Oh, they all say that. What else have you taken?'

'Nothing, just the money,' he mumbled.

'What?'

Gunno was afraid he might cry. 'I only took the money – that first time. I haven't taken anything else.'

'What's your name?'

'No,' said Anne quickly. 'I don't want to know his name.'

'Why, for God's sake? He's broken into our house, made himself a key, by the sound of it, come back when it suited him and driven you demented. We've got every right to know his name. It's a police matter.' He blocked the doorway as he said it, as if he expected Gunno to bolt.

But Gunno showed no signs of bolting.

'He could have got away any time, Geoff. He stayed and talked to me, answered my questions, sat on the well ...'

'On the *well*?'

'Yes. I wanted to see how he looked there, how I could have thought ...'

'He's very like him,' said Geoff, talking about him as if he weren't there. It's no wonder you thought ... But of course ...' He hesitated, then said his son's name slowly, as if it had become strange to him. 'Hugh would be two years older by now. He wouldn't look the same as he did then, same height, same build. It's nearly two years, Annie.'

Geoffrey walked over to the stove, brushing past Gunno, again as if he weren't there. Gunno could hear the clink of the cup coming out of the cupboard and the filling-up sound of the tea being poured. 'And from the back, Anne, I would have thought so too.'

Gunno picked up the note of regret in his voice. He could see it was important that he'd stayed. What had Geoffrey said to her? That she'd been 'hallucinating': that was it. He'd thought she was crazy.

'Could I go now?' he asked dully, pulling the key from his pocket and giving it to Anne. Behind him Geoffrey banged his cup down on the counter. 'Yes, go, for God's sake go,' he said. 'And make sure you don't come back.'

He could hear Anne's voice, low, saying something as he moved out to the back verandah and opened the wire screen door, and then Geoffrey's voice, raised. 'Sentimental claptrap. The boy's just a common thief.'

Gunno stopped at the deli on the way home, as he'd been asked to do in his morning letter, and got two pies for tea. It seemed a funny thing to be asking: 'Could I have two cold pies please?' as if it mattered, as if anything would ever matter again. They always got cold ones so that they could heat them up fresh for tea. Often Gunno would make a salad to go with them.

He thought of pulling out the vegetable bin, taking out the lettuce with its various shades of green, the tomatoes, green pepper, a carrot, and putting them on the sink ready for washing. He would get out the colander then and a clean tea-towel for drying everything off. He thought about each stage of this as he rode home. That would fill in some time. He could water the garden too. The lawn was looking dry again and some of the bushes were wilting. It was going to be a hot summer. They had had so many hot days already. He thought about the watering and the weather. When he had done the watering it would be almost time for his father to come home.

There was one thought that he was clinging to, like a drowning man to wreckage: one thought that could still arouse his interest where everything else was blank. It had to do with his father. There was something he had to ask him. It was a long time since he had talked to his father about anything much, let alone anything important. He'd have to watch for his moment.

But it came, after tea. His father leant back in his chair, wiped some crumbs from his mouth and smiled. 'Got a bit of back pay,' he said confidentially.

'Much?'

'Guess.'

'A lot?' Gunno could see from the wideness of his father's smile that he thought it was a lot. He didn't want to take away from his father's pleasure. 'Twenty dollars?'

'More than twice that,' said his father triumphantly, pulling out the money that he had kept separately in his wallet. He counted it slowly, smacking each ten down on the table. '$47.34!'

Gunno tried to look impressed. He thought of the money the gang had often had, lying thick, after a raid.

'Why don't we celebrate?' said his father. 'What about a film and tea in town on my next Saturday off?'

'Great, Dad.'

His father smiled and went over to read the paper in an easy chair. Gunno followed him.

'Dad.'

'Mm?'

'When we lived in Melbourne . . .' He waited for his father's eyes to leave the paper. He knew they would. He wanted to see his face when he said it. '. . . and Mum went away,' he said with a rush, 'why did you say she was crazy?'

'Oh, I didn't say that.' His father's face took on the shut look that it often had when he mentioned his mother. Now he flipped his paper as if he meant to go back to it.

'She was in one of those places,' said Gunno.

'Look, son, they're just hospitals, like anywhere else.'

'But you said she was crazy: you sent her there. She didn't want to go. She was crying.'

'The doctor thought it was a good idea; she was tired, she needed a rest.'

'Why?'

'*Why*? Why does anyone need a rest?' His father was getting more annoyed. He would have to be quick.

'I mean, why did he think it was a good idea? *What was she doing*?'

'Keep your voice down, Gunno. I've told you about it all before.'

‘Tell me again – *please* Dad.’

‘Well, she’d get upset about nothing, and she’d get one thing into her head and go on and on about it.’ His father paused. ‘And, of course, she always said she could predict things – and see into the past, that sort of thing. And then . . .’

‘And then?’

‘She started seeing things.’

‘What kind of things?’

‘She said she could see people, when no one else could.’

‘What do you mean?’

‘People who weren’t there.’ He hesitated. ‘People who were dead, Gunno.’

He put his paper down. ‘Like old Mr Watchman who lived next door. She saw him in the street with his old dog six months after he died.’

‘The dog?’

‘No, Mr Watchman. After he died the dog hung around and people fed it. We fed it sometimes. The house was empty a long time but the dog stayed. You’d see it in the garden. Remember the tiny gardens, Gunno?’ His father’s eyes lit up as he remembered. ‘There was that old skimpy hedge with the shiny leaves. The dog’d lie in there and sometimes on that patch of tough lawn – buffalo, I think it was – or on the verandah. Old Mr Watchman painted it green one day “to take the dead look off the cement” he told me. But it didn’t, for that was where they found him not more than a week later with the dog whining beside him. Painting it in the heat had been too much for him. I’d offered to help – he could hardly bend over to do it but he said he already had someone helping. He meant the dog. It was one of those white dogs with the black patches over its eyes. It never left him.'

Gunno thought about the old dog, staying on. 'What happened to it in the end?'

'Oh, it just drifted off when the new people came,' said his father, losing interest.

'And you mean Mum got locked up for seeing Mr Watchman trying to look after his dog?'

'No one ever locked your mother up, Gunno. And he was *dead*. Haven't you been listening? Your mother's just one of these people who can't cope with ordinary life and invents things, maybe, to make it bearable. It hurt her to think of that old dog . . .'

'Mr Watchman and who else?'

'What?'

'You said "people". People who weren't there.'

'I can't remember,' said his father shortly. Then Gunno could see him making the effort to be patient. 'She was fanciful, Gunno. Remember how she'd be reading all the time. Remember how much she used to read to you.'

'That doesn't make her crazy.'

'No one's saying crazy,' said his father, picking up his paper again. 'Unbalanced, perhaps.'

'That's just another way of saying it,' said Gunno bitterly. 'Like "hallucinating".'

'*What*?'

'You've let me think . . .'

'Look, Gunno, I haven't let you think anything. I work hard, I hold down two jobs so that I can send your mother money and keep us going. I do – I've done my best.'

Gunno went to bed and stared at the ceiling. It seemed very white and smooth and vacant. He searched for a crack or even an insect, but it was blank, formless. He thought he would have to stare at it all night, but he woke with the light still on and the sun streaming in and the memory of a dream.

He tried to think of it before it would dissolve in the light. In the dream he'd been a little boy. He could tell he was small because he couldn't see over the hedge yet he knew it was important that he should. He tried to climb it but there was nothing to hang on to and he got scratched and kept falling back again. He called for his mother but she couldn't come. The hedge was growing now, higher and higher. He tried to crawl under it and he could just see through it the verandah and somebody lying on it, wrapped in a hammock. He pulled himself through and crawled across the lawn and a huge dog bounded out of nowhere snapping and snarling. But just as he started to scream the dog licked his face and Gunno could see that it was Sam.

Chapter Seventeen

The days passed, long and hot. School was over for the year: indeed the holidays would soon be finished. Christmas had passed almost without Gunno noticing it. He always hated Christmas now anyway, alone with his father. He hadn't seen any of the gang, except once in the distance: Jess and Pete on their bikes, heading, he thought, for the beach.

All the days seemed to be hot. Today was to be exceptionally so, over forty degrees, he read in the paper. But he would have known it from the sky of the evening before. Little ridges of pink cloud had lain in broken bands everywhere across a blue sky. And then, as the blue had paled, the pink glowed through it like the fire colour in an opal.

Normally, on a day as hot as this would be, he would have gone to the beach, but he had developed a fear about it: a rather absurd fear that if he went there he would see Jess. But if he couldn't go to the beach he would have to go somewhere. He packed his haversack with a drink bottle of iced water, two tomato sandwiches and *A Wizard of Earthsea*. It was Hugh's copy, but he didn't quite know how to get it back.

He wheeled his bike down to his gate, past the fence where Wally had wanted to have a fight, down the snaking part of his road that bordered the park, down to the main road. He avoided looking in the direction of the big house, and turned south, heading up the steep winding road towards Clarendon. He and his father had bought fresh rolls there one day. He had a vague thought that that would give some point to his ride.

It was steep – too steep a direction for his bike and he'd have to push it part of the way. And it was too hot a day already for either cycling or walking. Stepping out into the air had been like walking into a dry hot bath. He settled his old navy towelling hat firmly on his head and trudged up the long slope.

He walked on the inner side of the road, although it was the left side, for here there was scrub and some comfort from the straggly gums. The other side fell sheer in gold-burnt grass that stretched in folds to the dancing blue of the reservoir and beyond it, the sea. Sweat trickled down inside his navy singlet and settled in the backs of his legs. He took his hat off briefly and pushed his hand up under and through the thick hair at the back of his neck. It was already damp and sticky.

The road flattened out at the Cherry Gardens turn-off – high up but flat. He turned round, still sitting on the seat of his bike but with his feet on the road and looked back the way he had come. The sky was misting over and the hot ball of the sun peered eerily through it. It reminded him of the day at the beach when he had gone early and met Jess that first time. 'I don't mind being alone together,' she had said.

The reservoir and the sea, so shimmering and blue only minutes before, lay grey and still. All the life seemed to be leaching out of the day for the birds had disappeared too and the bush lay silent. Everything had a waiting feeling. We're heading for a change, he thought, perhaps even a storm. He thought of rain drumming down on their garden (still parched-looking in spite of the bit of watering they had managed to do) making holes in the sand, splashing into the sea, into the grey quiet reservoir below.

Then he noticed that although it was so still on the ground, something was happening in the air above. The gum trees were starting quite slowly to move their crests. But as he watched, the movement spread lower and whole trees began to sway and bend. The wind was rising but not freshening. It was from the north, a hot wind, bringing dust. And now the leaves lying thick beneath the trees started to lift and dance, slowly at first, then whipping up. One of them smacked him on the cheek as it blew past. His eyes were starting to sting and he could taste grit in his mouth.

Perhaps I should go back, he thought, but he went on, past the turn-off to Cherry Gardens. He could cycle now, on a flat, then a downhill stretch. The road twisted and bent and dust blew up and leaves swirled around him as Gunno pedalled mechanically on. But he stopped at Sugar Loaf Road. The sun beneath the white clouding mist had turned to an ominous red, and the mist was settling lower, starting to blot out the hills and dips around him. Gunno looked at it, half aware, as though it were a painting. He would have to go back. And the wind was gusting against him now. It would be easy to go the other way.

He turned his bike and rode back to the start of the road that wound steeply down into the valley: the road that he had just climbed. But at the last minute he turned right, taking the winding road to Cherry Gardens. He had half an intention to do more than that too – the road, he remembered, ended on Rutland Hill. There had been something in the paper that morning that had made him think very clearly of Hugh: something to do with the date, was it? He would ride home that way, completing a circle. It would pass the time. Besides, he thought he would quite like to see how it would look on such a day, with dust swirling and the trees bending almost to the ground.

He stood up on the pedals, his face stinging, and battled against the cross-wind, cycling through the dips and rises of the road past the Cherry Gardens farms. He looked for the raised-up letters in the hedge near the post office – 'Cherry Gardens' they said: now he knew he was on the stretch of road that led past the golf course and came out at Rutland Hill. When he reached it he turned left and pedalled, quite slowly now, down to Woodsman's Drive and the land below it.

The dry storm made everything look weird, and the land beside the pylon was no different. He wheeled his bike in through the gap in the fence and left it, with his haversack, under the small distinctive clump of red gums that he had noticed on his last visit. The wind was taking the tops of the trees and beating them into one another. Gunno thought of how it had looked that other day: so peaceful, the sun rippling through the leaves like water, the forest of eucalypts stretching in deep slopes as far as he could see. Now the ugly, blood-coloured mist blotted out the blue smoke of distance.

He crunched his way down the slope over piles of twigs and branches, over crisp dry leaves. But there was something different – surely there was. He shook his head and looked for a familiar landmark. He must just have taken a slightly different track. But no, he was sure this was the angle he had come in at: there was the native cherry grove to the right and the first pylon to the left, and the waterhole . . .

He looked through the haze for its steep red dirt sides and for the circle of muddy water. His eyes swept the area below the native cherries in a casual and then in a concentrated way. He stared in disbelief. It wasn't there. And the fallen red stringy that he had sat on, looking into it, it wasn't there either. He looked above where it had been for the two hugely tall yet thin red stringys with the frail waving top knots of foliage that had reminded him of giraffes. He looked up – but where two trees had stood, there were now three: three very tall trees with reddish straggly bark, not two as he had remembered.

Chapter Eighteen

Everything seemed to be taking on the queer half-logic of a dream. Even the trees were slightly out of focus, slightly distorted. Gunno had stumbled further into the bush, past the blackberries to the ledge where the flat area suddenly stopped and another steep, much steeper slope began. He had sat down on a stump, grey like driftwood with the inside worn away in circles like a crater, and shut his eyes. He had reached for his hat, to pull it over them, and found that he had lost it. It must have blown away on the road somewhere or fallen off where he had left his bike. Not finding the waterhole had upset him; but he must have come in at a different part of the fence. That was the logical explanation. But then there was the pylon wire, stretching above him as it had been before. It *must* be the same spot.

He looked around him for some normality: something to grasp that was the same. The mist had cleared by now – had lifted as if it had never been. The blue wrens were the same, flitting and darting among the native cherries; the rosellas were the same, sending their clear calls like sword blades through the clearings; the fresh smells of eucalypt were the same. But that was strange too – after so much dust, after so much grit in the air.

Yet . . . Gunno stared at the trees, at the shrubs. It seemed to him that the trees were lower and the understorey higher than he remembered. But that was madness. Even the *sun*. He looked at his watch. The sun should have been higher up at this time. But there it was, slanting through the trees, noticeably dropping.

Gunno put his hands out in front of him to see if they were trembling, then he felt his forehead for heat: perhaps he was catching a flu out of season. But he felt perfectly normal – even cool. Everything *was* perfectly normal. He tried to make his thoughts reassuring, forcing himself to look in a mild way up through the scrub towards the flat area of pasture that fronted the main road.

It was then that he heard it: the distant crackling noise of something or someone pushing a way through the scrub. He narrowed his eyes, focussing up towards the road. And then he saw him. There was a boy walking briskly through the undergrowth as if he were used to doing it and sure of his way: a boy wheeling a bike, a green bike rather like his own but that glittered with newness where the sun fell on it.

He stared at the figure and felt himself tremble. This was a weird day, and a weird place, but weirdest of all this figure with the bike. Yet ordinary too, ordinary and even familiar – too familiar. Walking relentlessly towards him dressed in dark jeans, white and blue joggers like his own and with a red parka slung across his shoulders was a boy of about twelve: a boy like himself.

Gunno felt sick. He waited for the figure to approach him and then somehow blend into him, merge with him. But of course it didn't happen. The boy wheeled his bike away from him, over towards the native cherries and dropped it, noiselessly, into the thick mat of scrub. The blue wrens, disturbed, flew off up the hill. The boy turned then and walked past Gunno, through the hakea bushes and cup gums, not seeming to see him.

It was then, of course – so slowly the thought came to him that he knew he must be dreaming and that all the other strangeness was part of this same rich dream – it was then at last he realised: this figure, this boy with the parka and the glitteringly new bike, this boy, so like himself – this boy could only be Hugh.

Gunno shut his eyes: he must be imagining it. When he opened them there was no sign of the boy, no sign at all. He sighed, relieved. Having so much imagination was often a curse. He had been thinking about Hugh far too much lately, that was all. And then in the paper that morning there had been something . . . He looked around him, thankfully, at the sanity of the black-trunked wattles and thought of Wally, of the graveyard. There in August the wattle hung rich over the fence, cascading down beside Wally's favourite grave.

He got up and walked around, taking great gulps of air. Twigs broke beneath his feet; rosellas flew off shrieking. Yet, in spite of himself, he knew his eyes were searching all the time, searching for a glimpse of . . . And there at last he saw it – a splash of red. The boy was far ahead, pushing his way through thicker and thicker understorey. Carefully, slowly at first, Gunno started to follow him, and then faster, as he was aware of the boy getting further and further away. He stumbled over a fallen branch of wattle and nearly fell. Now the boy had disappeared altogether. He couldn't even hear the crack of twigs beneath his feet. Gunno drew himself still and listened, but he could hear nothing. Panic filled him. He rushed forward, not caring about the noise, broke through some straggly hakea bushes and looked around him.

He had come to a clearing, a very green place at the bottom of a sharp new rise. The rest of the scrub was grey, washed out, but this part was different. Bright green mosses covered the low-flung rocks; native grasses sprouted everywhere. Gunno was so taken up with the greenness that at first he hardly noticed it – a small emptiness, a blackness, in a bank. But when he moved closer, idly curious, he could see what it was: it was a hole, an entrance even. He walked over and peered in. It was a tunnel, almost as high as himself and it led deeply into the hill.

It was going to happen then. What he had feared was going to happen. It hadn't just been in his mind, for here was the entrance, here was the tunnel, almost as he had imagined it. It was his dream: the terrible dream he had first had that peaceful day in the hammock; the dream that seemed to stem from *The Tombs of Atuan* yet had come to him before he had even opened its pages. He felt afraid, but only in a distanced sort of way as if over his fear curtains were drawn somewhere in his mind. He felt excited too: he could feel tingling in his feet, in his hands, then spreading all over him. He shivered and put first his hand, as if testing the air, and then his foot into the entrance.

Gunno stumbled along the passage, feeling the stony walls. The air was not stale, as he had imagined it would be, but thick with the smell of earth. With disturbed earth. This was where Hugh had gone – you could tell from the air. It was remarkably light still in the tunnel so it wasn't the dark that made him stumble. He couldn't believe that this was happening to him. Wait, he wanted to say to whoever arranged things. I'm not ready for this yet. I want to think about it. This is too important to be happening now. I need more time. He felt light-headed, even faint, and was surprised to find a taste of sick rising in his mouth. His jeans caught on a sharp edge of rock, then ripped as he pulled away. He stared at his leg through the tear. It was marked with white from the stone and blood was starting to ooze in patches from a graze on his knee. The pain shocked him – not that it hurt much but it convinced him that it was all really happening.

He stood still and thought about turning back. He even turned around to face the entrance. Outside, the bush had just seemed ordinary, natural, calm, but out of the darkness it stood framed like another world, a kind of paradise. Gunno stared at the native grass and cup gums, the hakeas and fireweed; most of all at the bright sunshine. No one was making him go on. He didn't need to follow Hugh into the hill.

Yet perhaps he could do something. Perhaps he could stop it all from happening. And clearly he *did* have powers like his mother. If only he had greater strength. People with powers but without great strength ended up sick or mad: cast aside like his mother. He would have to go on. Slowly, reluctantly at first, he walked up the darkening passage, the light turning to grey and then to darker grey. He could still see a little – there must be cracks in the roof, he thought, but everything was muted, shadowy. He shivered sometimes as he walked on.

Yet although he was moving so slowly he seemed to be catching up on Hugh. He could hear him now – echoing steps in the distance. A real boy then, who made a noise. That should have made him feel more comfortable, he thought, but instead he could sense the sickness rising from his stomach again. He clung to the rock face and sidled on. The passage was curving sharply to the left. He really was catching up – the noise was so loud now. But it was the other way round for as he reached the curve he had a confused sense of movement and flashing light and suddenly a torch beam shone straight into his eyes.

'And who might you be?' asked a grim voice. 'What're you doing following me?'

Gunno turned his face away from the beam.

'Come on, who are you? What're you doing here?'

Gunno tried to keep his voice level, but it shook as he answered. 'I saw you come through the scrub. I just wondered where you were heading.'

'Well, now you know, you can head straight out again. This is my place.'

He just spoke like anybody. It could have been Wally there. Somehow that made it worse. Gunno started to shake all over. But he had to answer him. He nearly said, 'It's just an old mine. It could be anybody's.' But he knew he had to be more tactful than that. He tried admiration. 'It's a super spot,' he said placatingly. 'No wonder you want to keep it to yourself.'

Again Hugh turned the torch beam on Gunno's face and then away. Then suddenly back. But he didn't say anything. Gunno leaned against the tunnel wall. He took deep breaths to calm himself. He had to make Hugh take him with him.

'How far does it go?' he asked. He would have liked to have the torch light shine full on Hugh – yet he was afraid of that too. He wondered what Hugh had seen. He seemed to be the same height that he was, the same build. Hugh appeared to hesitate, then he moved on, up the tunnel. 'I'll show you,' he said, but a bit morosely still, 'so long as you don't tell anyone.'

Now with the torch light ahead Gunno could follow more easily, which was as well because the tunnel was becoming steadily narrower and lower so that he had to bend almost double. He could feel his hurt knee protesting. Shadowy passageways branched off to the sides but Hugh kept following what must be the main tunnel further and further into the hill. The walls seemed to be of bluestone and every now and then Gunno could see a sharp indent. He ran his fingers along one. 'That's where they used to lay the gelignite,' Hugh called back.

Gunno longed to touch him – to prove that he was a real boy. He had to struggle to keep up with him for Hugh knew the way and where to put his feet, but as the passage turned again he caught up. He reached out his hand and touched Hugh on the shoulder. It felt real enough. Hugh wriggled away.

'What's up?' he said, sounding irritated.

'Where does that lead to?' asked Gunno, to distract him, hastily pointing to a narrow passage that veered away dangerously to the left. The floor of it broke off into jagged holes.

'Nowhere much,' said Hugh. 'You get in past these holes in the floor there' – he shone the torch to show Gunno more clearly – 'and there's a small flat opening and you can just slide through it if you breathe in. Come on, I'll show you.'

Gunno started to feel oppressed. Fear was filling the tunnel, was spilling out of him like lava out of a volcano. He stared at the jagged black holes. The whole place smelt of danger. 'Oh no. Thanks,' he said quickly. 'Don't you think we should stick to the main passage?'

Hugh stared at him. 'You're easy scared, aren't you? You stay here then.'

Gunno could hear the contempt in his voice but he couldn't care about that. 'I'd rather you didn't,' he said. 'Show me what's ahead.'

But Hugh was already stepping between the holes.

Gunno followed him, stumbling over the rough edges, feeling sick, feeling helpless, as he watched Hugh lie down and squeeze himself through the opening. He was almost there. Gunno sat down to wait.

'Are you really not coming?' Hugh was calling from the other side, giving him another chance. His voice sounded hollow, like a ghost's.

'Nup.'

'Yellow.'

'Maybe.' He would have to stay here in case it was here that it would happen. He rubbed his arms, finding them covered in goose flesh, then he sat rolled up in a ball, hugging his knees. He felt shivers run up and down his back. This *was* where it would happen. He could feel it in the walls, in the holes; he could feel it in the dark places of his mind.

Hugh was whistling on the other side of the rock. He was tapping at it, looking for silver maybe, looking for gold. Gunno shut his eyes in the darkness, dark on dark, and waited. 'I think you should come now,' he kept saying anxiously. 'Whatever are you doing?'

'Anyone ever tell you you're an old woman?' Hugh sounded amused now rather than angry. He started hammering at the rock with a large stone: he must have been – from the racket he was making. Then, in a pause between Hugh's hammerings, Gunno heard it: the merest sound, the merest suggestion of movement, a different feel in the air. But it was enough.

He scrambled to his feet. 'You've got to come now,' he shouted.

Hugh stopped hammering.

'Please, Hugh.'

There was no answer at first. Then, 'Aw, for Pete's sake,' Hugh said.

The sound was growing. Gunno couldn't keep still. 'Please, Hugh,' he said again.

And now Hugh was coming. First a hand, then an arm and shoulder started to appear on Gunno's side.

But he was moving so slowly – Gunno couldn't stand it. He grabbed him and pulled him through, scraping Hugh's arm and leg on the rough rock.

'For crying out loud,' said Hugh. 'You some kind of nut?'

But Gunno was looking upwards, listening. It was the same strange frail noise he could hear – a faint small singing sound – but now it was growing, changing. Or else there was another sound over it – a sort of creaking. And then he felt a sudden rush of air and almost at the same instant heard a great echoing bang on the other side of the ledge. The whole passage shook.

The boys stood still, waiting. But nothing else happened. Hugh bent down and peered in along the ledge. Dust blew in his face and he sneezed. 'Whew! It's a bloody great boulder!' he said. 'It's lying right across the opening.' He straightened up slowly.

So Hugh would have been trapped there, Gunno thought. His knees were collapsing under him but at the same time he felt a wave of pure happiness flow over him. It was a wonder, a miracle. He had saved him. What would his mother make of this! He thought of that empty, dusty room – filled again with Hugh. He thought of Anne. Somehow he didn't want to think of the little dog.

'Hey, you. Let's get out of this rotten passage.' Hugh was staring at him. 'And quit grinning. Okay, you were right. But tell me, how do you know my name?'

Gunno turned away and started back to the main tunnel. It was all right though. They were safe. He had saved Hugh. He could hardly believe it. He could have sung the words. But the name. Had he said Hugh's name? He tried to look vague as Hugh caught up with him and swung the torch light full in his face.

Hugh was impatient. 'Come on now. You called my name. It's why I came out.'

'You must have misheard. What name?' His mind rushed over words that could possibly have sounded the same.

'Hugh. You know very well. You said "Hugh".'

'"You", probably,' said Gunno with a tired shake of his head. 'I probably said, "Come on, you".'

'Maybe.' But clearly Hugh wasn't convinced. He thought for a moment. 'It isn't the way you talk. Someone who says "misheard" and "probably" doesn't say "Come on, you".'

Gunno thought of how Hugh might spell those words and had a sudden rush of affection for him.

'Why're you grinning like an ape again?' said Hugh. 'And how did you know anyway? You seemed to know something was going to happen.'

'I thought I heard something,' said Gunno. 'Some funny slight noise.'

'You must have ears like a dog,' said Hugh. 'My dog can hear people poke things in the letter-box and that's miles away from the house.'

My dog. Gunno felt a sudden pang. To think that Sam belonged to someone else, to this boy here. He thought of the little dog, thought of her welcoming Hugh, being glad to see Hugh, not to see Gunno, the substitute, the pale imitation, ever again.

'You're an odd character, do you know that? Look at the clothes you're wearing. You trying to be tough or something?' They were walking side by side now for the passage had widened and heightened. Gunno looked down at himself. He had on his jeans, sneakers, his navy tank top. Perfectly ordinary summer gear.

'Aren't you frozen?'

'It is a bit cold in here,' Gunno admitted.

'No, I don't mean that. Look at me: parka, jumper, skivvy. It was freezing today.'

Gunno remembered the heat as he'd ridden up to Rutland Hill. It had never been so hot. 'You're kidding,' he said, forgetting. 'It's going to be a scorcher. Forty degrees they said on the radio this morning.'

'You really are off your rocker,' said Hugh, starting to whistle and racing ahead. 'The best bit's still to come,' he called back. 'Wait till you see this!'

The passage was widening all the time now, and as it twisted round yet another corner it expanded into a huge room. Gunno could feel the sense of height before he could see it as Hugh swung his torch beam around. It reminded Gunno of a picture he had seen once of the entrance to a casino, where the roof rose, arching storeys high; the entrance was three or four times the normal height of such a room. This was where their tunnel met another – maybe fifteen or twenty metres above it, and where their roof became its floor, rough wooden planks were laid across it, blocking off jagged open rock. Perhaps it was more like a cathedral, Gunno thought, arching up but not to the sky – only to a higher bit of the hill.

'It's . . . big,' Gunno said ineffectually, not knowing how to put into words the strange effect that the place had on him – half cathedral, half . . . burial ground, he thought suddenly. And at once the twinge of unease he had felt as he followed Hugh further and further into the hill became a flash of fear, for now he had seen an ancient-looking rope hanging from the rafters and reaching almost to the ground. His feeling of fear centred on the rope. Perhaps it had all been too easy . . . the ledge . . . saving Hugh.

But Hugh's eyes were following his, were searching out what he was staring at. 'Good at shinning up ropes?' he asked. 'Let me show you. Then you do it.'

Gunno licked his dry lips. 'It's an awful-looking rope, Hugh. It could break. And it's tied on to those old bits of wood. They might be holding back ...'

But Hugh wasn't listening. He had already moved forwards and was reaching for the rope. Gunno rushed up to him and seized it from his hands. 'Let me try,' he said.

'Impatient, aren't you?' muttered Hugh, but he let him take it.

Gunno could feel his heart quicken as he lifted himself up by his arms and then pulled his knees up to their height. The platform of wood creaked ominously above him, and his grazed knee, stiffening now, protested. But he kept on. He could see Hugh staring up at him, shining the torch on his progress. He levered himself up onto the rough wooden platform and looked around him. The rock had been cut away here, and large loose boulders lay at what was really the end of a main passageway. He wondered why they had stopped here, for there was light coming from somewhere, enough anyway to see the gleams of white in the rock. Silver-lead, Gunno thought. His fear had left him now, and he enjoyed the sharp swing down on the rope, and was smiling as he joined Hugh at the bottom.

'Great, isn't it?' said Hugh. 'My turn, now.'

But at this, Gunno felt his fear return. Maybe Hugh was heavier – he looked it, although it might just have been the parka. 'Oh come on,' he said, feigning impatience, shepherding Hugh away. 'Show me the rest of the tunnel first.'

But there wasn't much left for Hugh to show him – only more of what was like the earlier part of the tunnel. It became narrow again with short passageways branching off, then it petered out, quite unexpectedly, after a sharp bend.

Hugh sat at the end of the tunnel with his back against the stone, panting. Gunno wouldn't sit – he thought if he kept standing he would be able to prise Hugh back more quickly to the sunlight. It seemed to be part of another world when he thought of it now – of the sunlight, the wind, the gums with the light rippling off their leaves like water. 'I'm starving,' he said.

'Bring anything with you?'

'Yes. In my haversack outside.'

'What you got?'

'Oh, this and that.' He was deliberately vague. If Hugh knew he only had two probably very over-heated tomato sandwiches he wouldn't be all that anxious to come.

'Mystery man,' said Hugh. 'Okay, let's go.'

Chapter Nineteen

Gunno felt a confused mixture of relief and fear as they hurried back down the tunnel. Surely nothing could happen now. He longed to break out into the sunshine. He tried to keep that image before him, but the rope in the cathedral room kept coming back into his mind, swinging in and out of his vision. He tried to chase it away. He tried to think of something else, for thoughts are powerful things, and could maybe lead towards what you wanted most not to happen. Yet as they entered the vast vault of a room with Gunno's mind steadfastly blank, Hugh's was full of the rope. His torch beam sought it out at once. 'I'll just . . .' he started to say, but Gunno grabbed his arm and pushed him urgently down the narrowing passage. 'Come on, I'm starving,' he said.

'You're a bit of a bully, aren't you?' said Hugh as Gunno rushed him down the tunnel. 'Although you don't look it. You look . . .' He paused, then seemed to decide not to say any more, about that anyway. 'Here, you go first, and I'll flash the torch ahead of you.'

The passage was narrowing still more, and Gunno had been stumbling and crashing into things because of the rough uneven earth floor and jagged rock edges. He'd trodden on Hugh's heels more than once.

Usually a return journey seems shorter than the outer

one because the way is known, Gunno thought. But this one felt longer, much longer. Gunno's excitement and dread came in bursts as he went ahead down the tunnel. He felt anxious that he couldn't see Hugh. 'You all right?' he kept saying, ludicrously, to the figure behind him.

Hugh laughed. 'I'd never need a nursemaid with you around. You're strange. Why should you care if I'm following you or not? You don't even know me. You'd get all the stuff in your haversack to yourself. You make me feel,' he said, after a pause, 'like that Greek legend. You know, about the man who went back to the underworld for someone. He could have her if he didn't look back.'

'Orpheus,' said Gunno. 'Orpheus and Eurydice.'

'Don't look back,' Hugh teased.

Gunno felt a sudden chill and then a longing to look back. But superstitiously he kept on, willing himself not to turn.

And then, as the tunnel rounded a corner and straightened out, he could see the sunlight. 'Doesn't it look great?' he called to Hugh without turning round. 'The outside, see it?'

Hugh pushed him down so that he could look over his head. 'It's because it's framed,' he said. 'Makes it look like a kind of paradise, doesn't it, but it's just ordinary calm old bush.'

Gunno started, to hear his own thought given back to him in words. He longed even more for the sunlight. He longed to see Hugh's face.

Yet when they got outside to the patch of green he didn't dare look at Hugh. His spirits were soaring wildly – he couldn't let Hugh see his face. He turned and ran up the slope. 'You stay there,' he said. 'Don't move. I'll be right back.'

'Okay, Grandma,' Hugh called after him.

Gunno ran through the scrub, tearing his way through bushes that on the way down would have made him go round, almost ready to fly with excitement. He had done it! He had really done it! He had saved Hugh. He had brought him out of the underworld as Orpheus had failed to do. He had altered time. He had changed the past. He had powers so great . . . He wondered what his mother would think, what she would say: if it would change things for her. He wanted to shout to the blue wrens above him in the native cherries. He wanted to shout out loud.

He grabbed his haversack, still lying near his old bike under the grove of red gums, and ran back down the slope. He didn't even notice his knee until he came pounding into the green clearing and threw himself down beside Hugh.

'You really *are* hungry,' said Hugh. 'You sounded like a wild bull tearing through that scrub.'

Gunno lay flushed, panting, looking up, in daylight, at Hugh.

The laughter died down in his eyes. Anne had been wrong. It was almost like looking at himself – the same pale skin, the dark eyes, the way the black hair grew. Hugh tossed his out of his eyes just as Gunno had an urge to do the same. Hugh was staring at him too. 'I thought so in there,' he said, 'but it was too dark really to tell. The torch picks out strange things sometimes. I thought I might be mistaken.'

'You mean . . .' said Gunno, then paused.

'We could be brothers,' said Hugh. 'We're like enough for that. We could almost be . . .'

'The same,' he might have said, Gunno thought, but whatever it was he held it back.

'What's your name?'

'Gunno.'

'Yes, it would be something outlandish like that,' he

muttered, but to himself. 'I always knew it would be a strange name.'

Gunno didn't ask him what he meant. He knew. He remembered that funny essay of Hugh's about his imaginary brother and the puzzle of his name. He must be thinking of that.

'Short for something?'

'For something but not really short,' said Gunno.

'I feel as if I've made you up,' said Hugh, shaking his head. 'It's odd, I was just thinking about you today – at least about your name ...' His voice trailed off. Then, after a pause while he kept staring at Gunno, 'Oh well, let's have a look at this lunch of yours.'

Gunno shivered as he undid the straps of the haversack.

'Hey, you're freezing,' said Hugh. 'I told you it was a cold day. Stick this parka on.' He laughed. 'Who's the nursemaid now?'

'Thanks.' Gunno's teeth were chattering, and Hugh still had a jumper. He pulled it on, then took out the battered sandwiches.

Hugh stared at the squashed, muddled-looking pieces of bread. 'How long you had these? Hell.'

'It's because it was such a hot day.'

'You really are cracked,' said Hugh. 'I know the weather changes but not like that.' He pulled one out of its greaseproof wrapping. 'Does feel hot,' he said. 'But that's crazy, too.' He looked at it thoughtfully. 'Live around here?'

'Not really. Well, in the valley. Rokeby Crescent.'

'That's funny,' said Hugh. 'I live just opposite. I take the dog up there through the park. I've never seen you. Been there long?'

'Oh, a while,' said Gunno, deliberately vague.

'Let's ride home together. Show me where you live.'

'Sure,' said Gunno, 'then maybe I could come back to your place.'

He wondered how he would explain to Anne, how he could explain to anyone what had happened. Still, he brushed that aside; that was the least of it. They would be so delighted to see Hugh he didn't suppose that explanations would matter too much.

It was Hugh who heard it first: a snuffling in the hakea bushes in front of them. The bush shook and then out burst an eager-looking black dog, waving its tail and slobbering. It ran into the clearing and bounded over to Hugh, plainly asking for a share of his lunch. It's a nice dog, Gunno thought, but not like Sam.

'I haven't seen you for a while, fella,' said Hugh, breaking bits off his sandwich. 'Here, you can have all of this. I may be hungry, but I'm not as hungry as all that.'

The black dog wasn't so fussy and each piece disappeared with an accompanying great gulp.

'You're a nice dog,' said Hugh, playing with its floppy ears, 'but you're not as nice as mine.' Gunno started. 'You know, when we went to get our pup,' Hugh said, turning to Gunno, 'we wanted a dog, so we said to the breeder a male pup, right. So we took him home. He's a hairy dog,' he explained to the black dog, 'not smooth like you. We never actually saw him cocking his leg in the garden but we never thought much about it either. We didn't realise till we took him to the vet to be desexed – and we'd called him Rob. Short for Robyn it had to be.' He laughed.

'I called her Sam,' Gunno wanted to say, but that odd feeling of desolation was on him again. Hugh had chosen the pup, had named her, had taken her to the vet. The dog was his.

The black dog decided there was no more coming from Hugh and nothing to be had from Gunno so it wagged its tail, circled the clearing twice, grinned widely and then disappeared.

'Where'd it go?' asked Hugh, after a while.

'Oh, could be anywhere,' said Gunno vaguely, but he rather thought that it had gone into the tunnel, so suddenly had it been there, and then not there. 'Let's go,' he said, anxious again. 'Let's get home.'

The wind was rising now and even with Hugh's parka on he felt the chill. His knee was starting to throb. He put the bits of greaseproof paper back in the haversack and fastened it up.

'Wait,' said Hugh. 'Listen.'

Gunno's heart dropped. There was a hollow sound coming out of the hill. It was the blasted dog, howling.

'Silly thing's got lost or stuck somewhere,' said Hugh. 'Can't be far. I'll just run in for it.'

'*No!*' Gunno's voice came out as a shout. 'You're not going in there!' He threw down the haversack and swung a punch to stop him but Hugh ducked and ran off.

'You really are crazy,' he yelled back.

Gunno followed Hugh along the tunnel. This time there was no torch to help him, yet he was almost running through the growing darkness. The light turned to smoky grey as he knew it would and then to dark. The sick taste was back in his mouth and his heart felt shrunken and fragile as if it were exposed to air. It was like a nightmare, he thought, where you couldn't get out of somewhere. Whatever he did, he ended up back in the tunnel chasing Hugh. But it would be all right, he thought. It had to be after all this. They'd get the dog – silly thing – and be back in the valley in no time. His dad would be getting anxious if they didn't. It was sure to be getting dark soon.

But when he found Hugh it was in the vast vault-like room. Hugh was standing, staring helplessly up at the black dog who was howling equally helplessly down from the rafters above.

'How the heck could it have got up there?' asked Hugh. 'Could hardly have shinned up the rope.'

'Maybe he's scrambled up the side,' suggested Gunno. 'Or wait, I did notice it was pretty light up the top. Maybe he squeezed through from the outside somehow.'

'Anyway, however, there he is.' Hugh's voice was gloomy. 'What a stupid mutt. Oh well, nothing else for it.' And he swung himself up on the rope.

Gunno tried to rush forward, but he seemed able only to move slowly like a figure in a dream, so that by the time he reached the bottom of the rope, Hugh was already almost out of reach. He could perhaps still have caught him, but he was afraid to. Afraid of the double weight on that elderly rope.

'Hugh, come down at once,' he called.

'You sound like my dad,' said Hugh, 'but I don't have to take notice of you.'

He was still clutching the torch and as he swarmed up the rope the beam fell on the walls, picking out white flecks that glistened. The dog had stopped howling now, and was standing, his four feet close together on the frail-looking timbers, staring, head down, at Hugh's bobbing head. Panting, Hugh pulled himself up.

Oh God, don't let it happen, Gunno prayed. Whatever it is, don't let it happen. Or let it happen to me – I'd be safe, I don't belong here.

'What are you meaning to do with that mutt?' he called up. 'See if you can chase him out the opening. There must be one – see how it's light there, over on your left.'

Hugh looked vaguely in that direction. But clearly he wasn't going to bother. 'Would only be a crack,' he said. 'I've never seen anything. I'll just bring him down with me.'

Hugh was patting the dog, getting him used to him again, calming him down.

No, Gunno thought to himself. Oh no. He thought of the old rope, of the rotten timbers, the stone behind.

'No, you mustn't!' he shouted up, his voice cracked and urgent. He grabbed the rope. 'I'll come up and find the hole.'

'Really, Gunno.' Hugh's voice was amused. 'You should have yourself seen to. I've never known such a bundle of nerves. Now get off the rope. We're coming down.'

And with the dog clutched in his arms and the torch hanging out of his drooping hands, Hugh left the platform and swung out into space.

There was a sudden crack as the wooden platform tore away, and then a hollow rumbling. Gunno heard it at the same time as he saw Hugh float out into space with the dog, both of them outlined in golden light from the torch. The walls of the stone room and the arch overhead were stretching, were elongating themselves as in some sort of nightmare.

'Hugh!' Gunno called despairingly, hunching himself up instinctively as the dust, the stones, the rocks of his nightmare began steadily to fall. He could feel himself sinking, falling to the ground, and was aware of a kind of grey fog or smoke all around him. He thought once, in a distanced sort of way, that he could hear a dog whining, but he wasn't sure and it didn't seem to matter now.

Chapter Twenty

Gunno awoke to find dust in his mouth and grit on his face and one leg bent painfully underneath him. He turned himself over very slowly, miserably, and lay flat in the darkness. His head hurt now as well as his leg. He moved again cautiously. Maybe he was just bruised. He thought he had never seen such darkness: he shut his eyes but when he opened them it was just the same.

Then a vague thought came into his mind but went again before he could grasp it. The idea came and went, he thought, like a swinging rope. The rope! That was it, and the boy on the end of it. What had happened to Hugh? And to that silly dog – blast it! He tried to sit up but found that he couldn't. He peered into the darkness. He was getting used to it now. But there was no sign of the rope. He gazed in despair at the piles of shadowy grey rocks that lay everywhere across the earth floor.

'Hugh,' he called out hoarsely, but without hope.

The sound settled into silence. He tried again. And then, miraculously, out of the darkness came Hugh's voice.

'I'm here, Gunno, over here. I'm lying here. I can feel myself lying here and I can see the rock on top of me but I can't feel it, Gunno. Why is that? Am I paralysed?'

His voice was clear, strong even, coming out of the

rock. Gunno felt a rush of pleasure followed by sudden fresh pain and a strange realisation. And it was he who spoke with difficulty, for now it was his own chest that felt as if it were being crushed by the load of rock. He could feel his legs as if they lay inert under the rubble, yet he knew at the same time that he himself lay free.

'No, you're not paralysed,' he said.

The weight seemed to be increasing. He knew that Hugh was watching him, was feeling puzzled. He would be thinking that Gunno had seemed quite decent until now, but here he was lying free but inert, leaving him to lie under the rubble. Maybe he would think that Gunno was afraid to move in further.

'Are you okay?' he asked at last.

Gunno replied through set teeth. 'Sure,' he said shortly.

'Well, do you think . . .' Here Hugh hesitated, not liking to put into words perhaps what Gunno should have seen for himself. 'Do you think you could move some of this stuff off me? It's not hurting, but still, it should be, and I'd be happier with it off.'

The sides of the stone room were tilting around Gunno. He turned his head in the direction of the voice but the whole vault seemed to be misting over with darkness. He could feel beads of perspiration breaking out on his forehead. He could even feel that they were beads. He tried to lift up his hand to wipe them away but it lay still at his side, as motionless as if it were buried in rock. But Hugh was waiting for his answer. 'If I could, I would,' he said at last.

'Something must have hit you, Gunno.'

Gunno could hear the concern in his voice, but the voice sounded as if it were coming from far away.

'Maybe on the head,' Hugh went on. 'I thought you'd got away with it. I could see you there, lying clear. I thought . . .'

Gunno pulled all his strength together and half crawling, half rolling, he moved over nearer to Hugh. He pulled himself up, with his leg stretched straight out in front of him, and put his hands on the boulder that lay across Hugh's chest. But without the leverage of his legs he had no hope of lifting it. Even with all his strength. He moved some of the smaller pieces away from Hugh's legs. Only his face and one arm were showing out of the rubble. He tried again to lift the boulder.

'It's no good,' said Hugh. 'You'll just have to go for help when you feel better. I've got the torch.' He was gasping now, sounding awful.

'What happened to the dog?' asked Gunno.

Hugh began, suddenly, to cry. 'He's underneath me,' he said.

'Blast the stupid dog!' said Gunno, at the same time thinking of how it had grinned at them so cheerily before going off. 'I'd got you out! You were safe. I'd got you out!' His hands were tearing at the rubble, tearing at the rock. He seemed to be crying too.

Hugh's voice was quiet when it came. 'You're a mystery, aren't you? What do you mean, you'd got me out? Oh, the ledge. It's more than that, though, isn't it? You might as well tell me now. You'd been following me, hadn't you? You might as well tell me. Give me something crazy to think about.'

The pain had lifted now from Gunno but it seemed to have settled more deeply on Hugh. Gunno knew there was no more he could do. His own leg was broken, he thought. Certainly he'd never get out for help with it like it was. And it would take too long. Hugh was an optimist – clear water where Gunno himself lay dark. But Hugh wouldn't . . . And even if he could somehow have got to the outside of the tunnel, he could never get up through the undulations of the scrub. And it would be night-time by now. And thinking of the night a terrible thought came to him. He suddenly remembered the date of the morning's paper and realised why it had seemed important: it was the day before the date on *The Tombs of Atuan.* 'To Hugh, with all our love . . .' Tomorrow – oh God! – tomorrow it would be Hugh's birthday. No wonder he had been thinking about him even more than usual. That was why, without quite knowing it, that was why he had come to Rutland Hill.

At least now he could tell him a story. Gunno reached into the pocket of his jeans and pulled out the photograph of the scrub with the pylon wire in the corner – 'My Place'. He wiped his hands on his jeans and rested the photo on the boulder. He shone the torch on it.

'But that's mine,' said Hugh, amazed. 'How'd you get that?'

'From your room,' said Gunno. And at once he got a vivid shot of Hugh's room: the desk, the shelves, the red blinds with their moments of coolness, of pure blue. He clung to the image as of somewhere safe. He tried to explain about the room, the dust on the books, the musty smell, the door that was always shut; and that meant explaining about the gang and how they had come that first day to rob the big house. It seemed to involve telling Hugh, in a muddled way, about Geoff's music and videos, Anne's poetry and coffee mugs, even about the plant with the flowers like ballet dancers and what had happened to it. He went on and on, ignoring Hugh's astonishment, even anger, telling him about how he had lain in the hammock and sat on the well, and how in the end Anne had caught him in the house. He told him of how he had searched for the scrub and the pylon of the photograph, and of how Wally had helped, and of how he had come here through the dust-storm that day. It seemed to involve more than he wanted to say. But he said nothing about the dog.

'You're nice,' said Hugh at the end of it. 'And you

sure have a vivid imagination. I really like you, and you look like me too which must be an advantage for anybody.' He tried to laugh, but winced instead. 'But you sure are crazy.'

'Maybe,' said Gunno, flinching.

'I mean, you make it sound as if I've been away for ages, and it's only been a day. How could you have done all that in a day?'

'I couldn't,' Gunno agreed.

Hugh shut his eyes. 'You trying to tell me a sort of time-travel story, eh? To take my mind off. You break somehow into my time ...' Then he was silent, as if thinking it out. 'It would explain your clothes,' he said, 'and that amazing tomato sandwich, but I'd have to be as crazy as you to believe it.'

'Guess so,' said Gunno wearily.

Hugh was turning his head from side to side as if in pain. Gunno took off Hugh's parka and slipped it under his head.

'Thanks,' said Hugh, trying to smile. 'Let's share the comforts around. Tell me more about the gang anyway. That bit at least sounded true. Although you certainly know my house – I don't get that at all.' He tried to turn away, as if from the whole idea of it. 'Tell me about this guy called Wally. I'd like to meet him.'

'Wally haunts graveyards,' said Gunno, and then could have bitten his tongue.

'Go on.'

'There's this grave of a fifteen-year-old, fifteen and a half,' he corrected himself, 'and Wally's sorry for him and wonders how he died. He plants things on his grave – between the cracks. Worries about the colour scheme, that sort of thing.' The prevailing colour scheme was white and yellow, he remembered. Mentally he planted different coloured ground covers in the cracks of Wally's favourite grave, then mentally took them out again.

'You're all a bit odd,' said Hugh, 'aren't you? What does the girl do in her spare time?'

Gunno thought piercingly of Jess. Jess, always so rational, always so clean and cool. His colour for her was green. But Hugh was waiting. 'Jess,' he said. 'I don't know, really. I haven't seen her for a while. She likes the beach. She ...' He had an instant picture of her, green-eyed and tranquil, wading carefully through the pools left by the tide. The cool image of Jess made his mouth feel suddenly dry.

Hugh seemed to have dozed off. He was breathing very heavily. Gunno sat watching him, flashing the torch on his face from time to time to check that he was all right. Sometimes he wiped Hugh's wet forehead with the sleeve of the parka. Sometimes he tried to lift the rock – but however much he strained, it was useless. After what seemed to be a long time Hugh spoke. 'You did seem very afraid.' And then, as if thinking about something quite different, 'You didn't say anything about the dog. My dog, I mean. Did you see her?' His voice was urgent.

Gunno nodded. He thought of her waiting for Hugh, all that time; and waiting now, maybe, for him.

'She's a super dog. Rob. Robyn.' Hugh tried to laugh. 'A jolly sort of a dog. Doesn't take to strangers though.'

'No,' agreed Gunno.

'But she would have been okay with you.'

'Yes,' said Gunno, looking away. 'She was.'

'Did you ever play ball with her?' Hugh was gasping now as he spoke.

'Always,' said Gunno. 'Up the stairs, mostly. All sixteen of them. She enjoys that best. She's like a toddler, isn't she? Always wanting to play. Always following you around.' He looked closely at Hugh. 'You'd better not talk any more: you sound awful.' Awkwardly he patted Hugh's hand.

'What I reckon is I did a good job of it,' said Hugh.

'A good job of what?' Gunno had to bend down to hear the words.

'A good job of making you up. My . . . imaginary brother.'

But Hugh's eyes were shut again. Gunno shifted around, trying to get comfortable without actually moving his leg. He was freezing and stiff. He rubbed first one arm and then the other and then his good leg over and over again. Hugh seemed to be breathing more easily now. He wished that he and Hugh *were* brothers. If only they could go back to that big empty house together. He had a sudden flash of the plum tree at Anne's study window, but with its cut branch restored. Yet somehow it all seemed very far away: the tree, the house, the room, even the dog. He tried to picture the little dog but for once his mind was empty, completely empty of images of her. And it was Hugh's dog after all. 'A jolly sort of a dog,' Hugh had said. Gunno wouldn't have described her like that – 'super', yes, but 'jolly', no – but then maybe, without Hugh, she had changed: become more serious, more sombre.

He shone the torch on Hugh's face, first gently, to the side, but then anxiously, full on. There seemed to be something different – something empty, ironed out about his expression. He's maybe passed out, Gunno thought. He picked up Hugh's hand but it felt strange to the touch and fell back when he dropped it. He put his hand on Hugh's forehead, but it seemed cold. He felt his own – it was flaring with sudden heat. 'Hugh,' he called out into the vast graveyard of a room, 'you're not going to pack it in? You're not going to pack up on me now, are you? I came to save you. Why else would I have got to be here?' Helpless tears started to run down his cheeks.

Then pain flared up in his chest as it had before, and seemed to spread from there all over him like a tide. The pain shone red against the black of the room. He felt himself swing in and out of consciousness. He thought of his mother, waiting for her letter. He thought of Anne, waiting for her son. He imagined the shut door open, the bedroom alive again with Hugh. He couldn't be . . . He wouldn't say it, not even to himself, for thoughts are powerful things. His breath was coming now in harsh gasps. He prayed that he wouldn't scream. The weight of rock seemed to have shifted back from Hugh to himself. He mustn't scream or he would wake Hugh, sleeping so peacefully there. But just as he felt he couldn't hold the scream in any longer he felt a wave of thick darkness pass over him. He lay still, his head turned towards Hugh, his mouth falling open, his black hair spilling raggedly over his face.

Chapter Twenty-One

Gunno seemed to dream, and into the dream came a familiar voice. 'Gunno! Gunno!' it cried, first in a distanced and then in a nearer way. As it came nearer, too, it seemed to be setting up an echo so that the whole hall – he seemed to be lying in an empty hall – echoed with his name. 'Gunno, Gunno,' came the cry again, and again the echoes took it up. He dreamt now that someone was bending over him, covering him with – what was it? – sand. That was it, of course. Now he knew where he was. He smiled in his sleep, then slowly moved his head. 'No, Wally,' he said, for it was starting to hurt, the weight of the sand on his legs. He was at the beach, of course, and Wally was threatening to bury him.

Almost lazily he opened his eyes, and it was indeed Wally bending over him, but an appalled Wally, his eyes staring at him like bright circles out of his pale face, and the whole beach lit by searchlights. Gunno struggled to sit up.

'Lie still, son,' said a voice he didn't recognise.

He lay back, staring up, seeing above him not sky but rough stone, and wooden planks hanging rakishly down. He shut his eyes and groaned.

'Gunno,' Wally said again, and this time Gunno could hear the tears in his voice. 'You hurt bad?' His voice was anxious, defeated. 'I rescued you, Gunno. I found you. You won't pass out on me now?'

Gunno looked up at him and tried to smile. 'I'll be okay, Wally. I'm always okay.' There was a touch of bitterness in his voice. 'I won't waste your rescue. Have you found Hugh?'

'Hugh? Who's Hugh?'

'The other boy,' said Gunno. 'The boy who was here with me. There's a dog too and a torch. You must be able to see the torch,' he said, feeling suddenly terribly upset that they couldn't see it. 'It was just there. It's Hugh's.'

Wally turned to the searchers behind him. His voice was sharp, excited. 'There's another boy somewhere. Called Hugh. They were trapped here together. There's a dog.'

'No sign of anyone else,' Gunno could hear one of the men say, but sounding worried.

Anxiously he tried to raise himself again. 'He's over there,' he said, trying to shout, but his voice could only have come out as a whisper.

One of the searchers had to bend down to catch what he was saying. 'You lie still,' the man said soothingly. 'If he's there we'll find him for sure. And the dog as well.'

The effort was too much for Gunno. He could feel everything fading away again into a dream. The last thing he remembered was Wally's hand on his face, brushing his hair out of his eyes with what seemed to be a very wet hand.

He woke again – this time on the stretcher, amazed to see blue sky over him. Perhaps it had been a dream; perhaps he *was* at the beach. But then he heard the echoing cry of the black cockatoos and saw Wally's face beaming at him from over the edge of the stretcher, looking strange out of Gunno's old navy hat. It hadn't been a dream. It all rushed back. It had happened. 'Wally,' he said anxiously, his voice croaking out uncertainly. 'Wally, did you get Hugh?'

The light seemed strong in the hospital room. Wally patted Gunno's hand lying above the sheet, but timidly as if it might bite. 'No, they didn't find him. Not at first, anyway. It was the bike they found, soon after you conked out on the stretcher. There was this old bike, buried under all that undergrowth that's there. One of the searchers stood on it and the mudguard cut his leg. That woman from the big house ...'

'Anne?' said Gunno. 'Anne was *there*?' He pictured her tall, pale, heartbroken yet again.

'Yes.' Wally hurried on, skating over it. 'She heard you havering on the stretcher. She said you looked so much like her son.'

'Hugh,' said Gunno.

'And when she saw the bike she nearly fainted. It was *his* bike, she said – Hugh's. I went back for yours, Gunno. I rode it home.'

'What happened then?' Gunno asked urgently. 'When she saw the bike?'

'Well . . . they looked in that tunnel again where you'd been and this time they did find him, or at least ...'

'Where was it?' said Gunno. 'The bike?'

'Near those trees that look like firs.'

'Native cherries, blue wrens,' said Gunno. 'It was such a lovely bike,' he added after a silence, gazing up at Wally's puzzled face. 'Yesterday it glittered in the sun.' He shut his eyes and started to cry.

His father came at night, after work, anxious and peering at him, restless and unsettled, worried by a hospital room. 'I rang your mother. She said she'd like to come over.'

'There's no need,' said Gunno stiffly. 'I've only hurt my leg. And Mum's got her new job.'

'That's what I told her. It's more than that, though, Gunno. They say you cracked your head.'

Gunno reached up his hand cautiously. There was a bit of a bump under his thick floppy hair at the front.

'You've to have lots of rest and not worry about anything. I brought you the newspapers. Thought you might like to read about yourself.' He put them beside Gunno so that he could see the headlines without turning his head.

Gunno looked at the top one. *Boys Found in Ancient Tunnel*, it said. Gunno stared at it, then turned away. There had been a picture too, of him lying on the stretcher. There was a clump of stringys on the left.

'I know,' said his father. 'I thought so too. Seems rather bad taste, that, to me. Bad for the boy's family. But you know what reporters are like. Do you want me to read it to you?'

'No.' His voice sounded more emphatic than he had meant it to be. 'Thanks, Dad. Not now. I'll look at it later.'

But he hadn't read it later. He could imagine what its dry paragraph would say:

AMAZING COINCIDENCE

A twelve-year-old Coromandel Valley boy was rescued yesterday from a disused mine in the Adelaide Hills. The remains of a second boy who disappeared from his home just two years ago were found at the same site. The boy, Hugh

Lethbridge, was the focus of an extensive search in the Coromandel-Blackwood area at the time. His parents, interviewed yesterday, said that they had no idea why their son had gone to that particular spot. The area, on Rutland Hill . . .

His third visitor, a few days later, was Anne. She had asked his father, first, if she could come – if Gunno would mind if she came. She stood in the doorway looking at him. Hugh had been rather like her, he thought: the same dark hair and unexpectedly pale skin, the same dark eyes. He waited for her to ask how he was or if she could sit down. But she didn't. She just stood there, looking at him attentively, and then she said simply, 'Thank you for finding him.'

'Please sit down,' said Gunno, as his father might have done, motioning her into the chair at the side of the bed.

'One of the men who helped with the rescue . . .' She was getting straight to the point. 'We know him, at least Geoff does. He said,' (she was trying to phrase it carefully, Gunno could see), 'he said that you talked of Hugh as if he had just . . . gone. Just then. That night maybe.'

'Yes.'

'He said you said there was another boy with you.'

'Yes,' he said again. There didn't seem to be anything else that he could rationally say. Irrationally he wanted to talk about the torch. He wondered if they had found the torch.

'Maybe you could tell me about it.'

'You wouldn't believe me.' He moved his head restlessly. 'It wouldn't make any sort of sense.' He paused, then voiced his greatest fear. 'You'd say I was crazy.'

'Try me,' she said.

So Gunno told her the whole story of what seemed to him to have happened that night and before it: of how he had found the photograph, and after it the spot; of how he had seen a boy about his own age walking through the scrub; of how he had followed him and of what had happened in the tunnel; of getting briefly outside it and seeing the dog. The dog stood grinning before him as he talked about it – a totally nice, ordinary black dog. His eyes misted over.

Anne sat silent through all of it. Then – 'They did find a dog,' she said. 'They found a black dog.'

She looked wonderingly at him. 'It all seems true yet so fantastic at the same time, and I've been thinking . . . they said you'd hurt your head . . . but it would have been such an amazing coincidence for it to happen anyway. Maybe this is easier to believe. And more comforting. I saw your real name in the paper,' she went on. 'Your friend called you something else – Gunny, Gunno, was it?'

'My friend?'

'Yes, a blond boy, a bit younger than you. He came to the house – said you'd disappeared – wondered if we'd seen you. He was terribly upset but not quite believing it – that you *had* disappeared, I mean. It's how we felt when . . . and then it was the same day, the very same day that Hugh . . . I'm sure he called you Gunno, but in the paper it was something else.'

'Yes,' said Gunno, but thinking of Wally. 'Perhaps it was.'

She looked at him intently, as if she were seeing him properly for the first time; seeing him, Gunno thought, as he was, not just as a faded version of Hugh.

'"Gunnar",' she said slowly, as if she had just remembered it. 'It's the name in the old Norse saga, isn't it? That Gunnar too loved a house – like you – and his love for it led him into danger. I always remember the part about him looking back and seeing the golden cornfields and the new-mown hay and knowing that he could never leave it. There was his dog too. Remember his dog? How he loved it?'

Gunno nodded. He remembered the dog especially, at least he remembered what Gunnar's enemies had done to it. He couldn't remember anything else about it – what it had been like even, or what its name had been.

'Tell me, Gunnar, what did you call the dog? Our dog, I mean.'

Rob, Gunno thought. Hugh had called it Rob. Thought it was a male pup. A hairy dog, not smooth. 'Well, Pooch mainly. Hound, things like that.'

'You didn't give her a name?'

Again the feeling of desolation. It had been Hugh's dog after all. A jolly dog. 'Yes,' he said slowly, 'I did. I know it seems silly because she's a bitch, but I always think of dogs being male and cats being female . . .'

Anne was nodding as if she understood.

'So I called her . . .'

'Yes?'

'I called her Sam. And after all, you had given her a male name too. Rob's a male name, even if Hugh said it could have been short for Robyn, for it wasn't, was it? He thought it was a male pup.'

'*What* did you say?'

'Hugh thought it was a male pup, and that was a real mistake, because he *really* thought she was a male, and I never thought that.'

Anne passed her hand over her forehead. 'Who told you that?' she asked quietly.

'Hugh did.'

'You didn't read it somewhere? In a diary maybe?'

'No. He told me when we were feeding the black dog.'

She stared at him, searched his face wonderingly, then said, after a long silence, 'It's true, then, all that you have told me. It must be true. How else could you have known?'

It wasn't long after that that Anne had stood up and walked to the door. 'You're getting tired,' she said. 'But you do realise, don't you, that it means a lot to me to know. It means even more to me to know that he wasn't alone. It's made it possible for me to think about it now. I'm so sorry, though, that you got hurt.'

Gunno felt once more, but in a subdued way this time, the rush of the air, the tumble of the earth, the dirt in his mouth. He winced, and as the earth settled, he saw again the water-world of leaves and swaying branches, the hills that smoked with distance, the pylons stretching, the brown of the waterhole that he had seen, restored, from the stretcher. 'I can't see what was the point of it,' he said, half crying from weakness and frustration. 'There wasn't any point. I thought I'd got to him to save him, and it didn't make any difference.' His voice was breaking. 'All I could do was be there with him. He died anyway.' There, he'd said the word. For the first time he'd said it. No one else had, either.

'But Gunno.' Anne was staring at him, amazed. 'I thought you realised. It made *all* the difference. You were there with him when he died.' There, she had said it too. 'Imagine how lonely he would have been. How frightened. He wasn't nearly so frightened with you there. Don't you see? *All* you could do? It's as much as any of us can ever do, and you did it for Hugh.'

He spoke through his tears. 'But I . . . I didn't really

want to go into the tunnel.' He tried to explain as honestly as he could. 'I was afraid I'd go crazy. But somehow I had to. Something made me.'

Anne opened the door and turned back to look at him. He knew now she was looking really at him, not tracing resemblances to her son. He could see that she had been crying too.

'Call it goodness,' she said, smiling suddenly at him.

Chapter Twenty-Two

Gunno was writing a letter to his mother: then he was going to the beach with Jess. He was having his usual trouble with it, but not for the usual reasons. He had made a couple of false starts and still didn't seem to be getting anywhere. He tried again.

Dear Mum,
I'm sorry I haven't written. A lot's been happening lately, as you've heard, but it's hard to put in a letter.

He shivered suddenly. 'Put it all behind you,' his father kept saying. Yet how could he? And this might only be the beginning. One day – but not now, not yet – one day he would tell his mother.

I've got this friend called Jess, he went on. *She's in my year at school and she's tall with green eyes and she's got the sort of face that looks good with your hair parted in the middle.* He put a stroke through the description. His mum'd immediately start to wonder why he was describing her. She might think he was – what was Wally's expression? – gone on her. *I've known her for quite a while,* (he was on his second page now), *but lately she's become my friend. She wrote to me when I was sick. We're going to the beach today and I'll post this letter on the way, out the front of the primary school. Jess's a lovely swimmer – very neat and fast.*

I also have a friend called Wally. He's younger than me but he's so sharp it doesn't matter. I hadn't seen him for a while but recently he's been coming round a lot. Sometimes we kick a football in the park, sometimes we go roller-skating. A couple of times we've been to the ice rink at Keswick and we're quite good at it already.

Well, that's all I can think of, Mum. Dad's well but tired as he often is. He scored the last bit out. *Hope you get the time to write to me. We're both pleased, Dad and me, about your new job. It sounds great. You'll like it in the bookshop – just remember to serve the customers.*
Love from
Gunnar

P.S. Have you read A Wizard of Earthsea? *It's a kid's book – not that you'll mind that – and great. Come to think of it I'm not sure that it* is *a kid's book. It's an anybody's book.*

P.P.S. I would like *you to read it. G.*

That seemed to be the easiest way to tell his mother, he thought – or at least to begin to tell her.

He put the letter in an envelope, stuck it down with a pleased sigh, and took a stamp from his father's wallet. Then he went into the bedroom and changed into his bathers. He looked outside. There was a bit of a breeze. He put on a shirt, packed his haversack with sunburn cream and his old blue hat and two tins of drink that he'd had in the freezer overnight, pocketed his letter, shut the door behind him, and cycled off with a light heart to pick up Jess.

It was still early when they got to the beach, for he'd been up since six to write his letter. The sand was fresh, untouched, and the water glistened in an early morning blue-grey. The tide was still far out, but there were little pools everywhere amidst the hard ribbed sand. The sky was a kindly blue with small fluffy pure white clouds floating across it. It looked almost too good to be true – like an advertisement for Australia that you might find, Gunno thought, in some dark city, stuck on the wall of a tourist bureau in London or Barcelona.

They splashed through the pools, disturbing the seagulls, then walked over the ribbed sand to the white sand above, that still had the cool of evening trapped in it. Gunno took his shirt off and saw Jess looking at his white skin. She'd be thinking how tanned Pete was.

'Here, turn your back to me,' said Jess, 'and I'll put some lotion on. You don't look as if you've been out much in the sun this summer.'

'I haven't,' he said.

'What were you doing? I mean, before . . . I didn't see you around.'

'Nothing much.'

'I was hoping I'd bump into you some time. I was going to tell you I decided you were right – about what you said, that day at the beach. We disbanded the HBS not long after that. We just did one more raid after the big house and that was it. We knew it was wrong.'

'I'm glad.'

They lay on their stomachs in the cool satiny sand, feeling it shift into their hollows, lie firm on their legs. The sun enveloped them, as though the beach were a warm tent. Gunno lay perfectly still, wondering how long it was since he had felt so happy, afraid to move even the tiniest bit in case it would bring the moment to an end. But he must have drifted off to sleep, for he heard Jess calling him as if from far away, and felt her shake him gently by the shoulders. He pretended still to be asleep so that it would go on.

'It's getting hot, Gunno,' she called. 'Let's go for a swim.'

They ran down to the sea together, then walked out slowly as the cold water rose agonisingly to their waists. It wasn't like being with Pete would be, Gunno thought. Pete would be splashing her by now, to make her go in, or even pulling her under or carrying her out to deeper water.

'You know,' said Jess, 'Pete's eyes change against the colour of the water. Yours don't: they're grey everywhere, grey here.'

Gunno wondered if that were bad or good. He looked out to the horizon. There was a sailing ship out there, with three masts. It would be the *Falie*, on a pleasure cruise. It often came down the coast, often on Sundays.

'Anne and Geoffrey are going away,' he said. 'They've decided to leave the house. Geoff always wanted to go but Anne wanted to wait.'

'Poor woman,' said Jess, scooping up water in her hands. 'Is the dog going too?'

'Anne asked me if I'd like to have her, but I said I wouldn't.'

Jess looked at him in astonishment. 'But you're mad about her,' she said, 'and she's certainly mad about you.'

'Yes, I know.' Gunno looked suddenly miserable. 'I wanted to. I wanted to have her and Dad wouldn't have minded, but you should have seen Anne's face when she offered. She looked sadder than anything. You see, it was Hugh's dog. It's all she'll have now she doesn't have the house.'

'She won't need a dog to remind her,' said Jess.

'I know. But she was only offering because she felt she should – she felt she owed it to me somehow. But she didn't. She didn't owe me anything. She's done a lot for me as it is.'

'What do you mean, she's done a lot for you?'

'She believed in me,' said Gunno puzzlingly, 'and she helped me write to my mother again.'

He waded out deeper so that the shock of the cold water wouldn't make him gasp when he finally let himself slip into it. Jess stayed where she was, staring out to sea.

'You know,' he called, 'how my real name's Gunnar.'

'What?'

'Gunnar.'

The space between them was widening. Jess slipped into the water and cut through the clear green after him.

'Guess what his dog was called? The Gunnar I was named after; the Gunnar in the story I told you about.'

Jess smiled and shook the water from her hair as she reached him. She could still just touch the bottom, but she kept rising off it. They stood together, their heads bobbing out of the glassy sea. Gunno pictured the little dog at the top of the stairs. She was my dog too, he thought, with sudden happiness.

Jess looked at his eyes. 'Steadfastly grey,' she said, as if she weren't changing the subject. Then – 'I guess,' she said, looking at his slow smile, 'I guess he could only have been called Sam.'

Epilogue

Gunnar and his friend Njal were real people, and Sam was a real dog. They all lived in Iceland a thousand years ago.

Gunnar was the greatest fighter in Iceland. He hated bloodshed but was forced to kill in self-defence. As a consequence he was condemned to exile. On his way to the ship that was to take him away from Iceland his horse stumbled.

He had to leap from the saddle. He happened to glance up towards his home and the slopes of Hlidarend. 'How lovely the slopes are,' he said, 'more lovely than they have ever seemed to me before, golden cornfields and new-mown hay. I am going back home, and I will not go away.'

As an outlaw anyone was entitled to kill him. One night his enemies killed his dog Sam and surrounded the house. He held them off for hours with his arrows but then his bow was damaged. He asked his wife for a strand of her long hair as a bow-string but she refused. He was finally overwhelmed and killed. He had wounded sixteen men and killed two others.

You can read the stories of Gunnar and Njal in *Njal's Saga* where you will also find the story of Sam. Gunnar's splendid friend Olaf the Peacock knew that Gunnar's life was in danger when he gave him three presents: 'I want to give you three gifts: a gold bracelet, a cloak that once belonged to King Myrkjartan of Ireland, and a dog I was given in Ireland. He is a big animal, and will make as good a comrade-in-arms as a powerful man. He has human intelligence, and he will bark at every man he recognises as your enemy, but never at your friends. He can tell from a man's face whether he means you well or not. He would lay down his life rather than fail you. His name is Sam.' Then he said to the dog, 'Go with Gunnar and serve him as well as you can.'

The dog went to Gunnar at once and lay down at his feet.

About the Author

Eleanor Nilsson first thought of the story of Gunno and Hugh after she saw an old rambling home near Adelaide, a house that seemed welcoming but elusive, and even mysterious. This is the house in *The House Guest.* The dog in the story is Lochie, Eleanor's own Shetland Sheepdog.

Eleanor teaches courses in children's literature and the writing of children's books at the University of South Australia. Her first book, *Parrot Fashion*, was published in 1983, and since then she has written a variety of books for children, including *The Black Duck* which was shortlisted for the 1991 Australian Children's Book of the Year Award (Younger Readers). *The House Guest* is her first novel for older readers and was winner of the 1992 Australian Children's Book of the Year Award (Older Readers), winner of the 1992 SA Festival Award for Literature (Children's Books) and winner of the 1992 Victorian Premier's Literary Award (Children's Books). She has also written *Writing for Children*, a guide for beginning writers.

Eleanor lives in Coromandel Valley with her husband Neil and her son Martin. Her daughter Catherine now lives in Perth where she is studying to be a vet.

MORE GREAT READING FROM PUFFIN

☆☆☆☆☆☆☆☆☆☆☆☆☆☆☆☆☆☆☆☆☆☆☆☆☆☆☆☆☆☆☆☆☆☆☆☆

Hero Allan Baillie

The Hawkesbury River has broken its banks and the children must get home before the black water overwhelms the bridges. Four hours later they meet in dramatic and terrifying circumstances, and one of them will become a hero. But which one?

A Children's Book Council of Australia Notable Book, 1991.

High Hopes Ursula Dubosarsky

Julia organises English lessons for her father at home, but little does she realise that her life is about to be turned upside down. Quietly, surreptitiously, Julia plots her revenge.

A Children's Book Council of Australia Notable Book, 1991.

The Watching Lake Elaine Forrestal

Bryn and his family have moved near a lake. But bulldozers have disturbed the sinister Min Min slumbering in the misty waters. Years ago, the Min Min lured a woman to her death . . . This time it has chosen Bryn.

Shortlisted for the 1991 WA Premier's Literary Award.

Aviva Gold Jean Holkner

Aviva Gold's father has a dream – an obsession which uproots Aviva and her family from their home in Australia to live in Palestine in 1935, half a world away. An absorbing novel.

MORE GREAT READING FROM PUFFIN

☆☆☆☆☆☆☆☆☆☆☆☆☆☆☆☆☆☆☆☆☆☆☆☆☆☆☆☆☆

The Green Piper Victor Kelleher

Two teenagers and an old man are lured by a strange melody and discover something bewildering and sinister.

Baily's Bones Victor Kelleher

Alex and Dee unwittingly become involved in a re-enactment of the past when they discover the bones of old Frank Baily.

Shortlisted for the 1989 NSW Premier's Literary Award. Joint runner-up in the 1990 SA Festival Awards.

People Might Hear You Robin Klein

At first, Frances accepts her aunt's new life and the mysterious temple with its strange beliefs. But as she uncovers its sinister secrets she realises she has to escape.

Shortlisted for the 1984 Australian Children's Book of the Year Award.

Games ... Robin Klein

When Patricia is invited to a party by Kirsty and Genevieve she can't believe her luck. But the planned party falls through and soon Kirsty's spiteful games are out of control and the girls are plunged into a night of terror.

MORE GREAT READING FROM PUFFIN

☆☆☆☆☆☆☆☆☆☆☆☆☆☆☆☆☆☆☆☆☆☆☆☆☆☆☆☆☆☆☆

Speaking to Miranda Caroline Macdonald

On her quest to discover the truth about her mother's death seventeen years ago, Ruby gradually uncovers the answers to her questions – and much more besides.

Shortlisted for the 1991 Children's Book Council of Australia Book of the Year Award for older readers and the 1991 New Zealand AIM Children's Book Award.

Playing Beatie Bow Ruth Park

The scary game of Beatie Bow throws Abigail back in time to the Sydney of a hundred years ago . . .

Winner of the 1981 Australian Children's Book of the Year Award. Now a feature film.

Things in Corners Ruth Park

A collection of spine-tingling stories, each with more than a hint of the unexpected – and a surprise for the reader at the end.

Bianca Joan Phipson

Who is Bianca, discovered rowing aimlessly on the dam? A tense and gripping adventure sensitively told by an award-winning author.

MORE GREAT READING FROM PUFFIN

☆☆☆☆☆☆☆☆☆☆☆☆☆☆☆☆☆☆☆☆☆☆☆☆☆☆☆☆☆☆

An Older Kind of Magic Patricia Wrightson

Beneath the earth are older things than perhaps we understand: as old as the ground in which they live, and part of it. Every so often they appear again above the earth to visit the world that once was theirs alone.

Highly commended in the 1973 Australian Children's Book of the Year Awards.

A Little Fear Patricia Wrightson

Rather than live in an old people's home, Mrs Tucker and her dog Hector move into a deserted and derelict cottage. But something makes Hector angry, something that worries the chickens, something that is trying to drive Mrs Tucker from the land.

Winner of the 1984 Australian Children's Book of the Year Award, the Observer Teenage Fiction Prize and the Boston Globe/Horne Book Award. Shortlisted for the Carnegie Medal.

Ash Road Ivan Southall

When their parents go off to fight the fire sweeping across the hills, the children of Ash Road are left to face their own danger by themselves.

The Wind is Silver Thurley Fowler

It's a year of change for the Robinsons and Jennifer, but when tragedy strikes the family, it is Jennifer who must take charge . . .

From the author of The Green Wind, *which was the 1986 Australian Children's Book of the Year.*